ONCE UPON A TUNE

One Young Man's Quest to Become a Jazz Saxophonist

A Story by Harrison Goldberg

HarriSong Press

All artwork by Harrison Goldberg
Cover image: *Jazz Saxophones*
HarriSong Press logo: John Simon Burnett

Page xv: "Happy Talk" lyrics from the musical *South Pacific*
by Rodgers and Hammerstein

Page 20, lyrics from "Out of Nowhere" ©1931 Edward
Heyman, music by Johnny Green

Book Design and publishing services:
Constance King Design

ISBN: 979-8-218-27176-3
Printed in USA

P.O. Box 1684
Gualala, CA 95445
HarrisonGoldbergArts.com

The Temptation of Jazz

In The Bass Clef, a jazz cellar club uptown in Harlem,
*the serpent-shaped horn called saxophone**
tantalized with hypnotic forbidden fruit while bass, drums and
piano laid down a sultry groove.

Beneath the floodlights, an impressionable young man, sitting
with his unlived musical destiny, heard the sound and
immediately recognized the voice as his own.

---

* The Saxophone was the invention of Belgian musician and inventor, Adolphe Sax (1814-1894).

In the Pocket

My music is the spiritual expression of what I am—
my faith, my knowledge, my being...
When you begin to see the possibilities of music,
you desire to do something really good for people,
to help humanity free itself from its hangups...
I want to speak to their souls.
~ John Coltrane

Wonderment

For my Mother, where the music all started.

*For my Father who shared his love of
reading and literature.*

*For my beautiful friend Marjie whose constant support
encouraged me to bring this work to fruition.*

and

*For all those cats passed on, celebrated and/or unsung
who inspire and keep the jazz music chain unbroken.*

This story is lovingly dedicated to you.

Jazz Saxes Walkin'

Happy talk, keep talkin' happy talk,
Talk about things you'd like to do.
You got to have a dream,
If you don't have a dream,
How you gonna have a dream come true?

~ 1949 "Happy Talk"
from the musical *South Pacific* by
Rodgers and Hammerstein

On one fateful summer's evening, the spirit of adventure answering the clarion call of jazz music led the teenage me to slip past a momentarily distracted doorman and into the Piccadilly Lounge, at that time our city's sole jazz club. To my hiding place in a darkened corner at the rear of the room, the seductive tenor saxophone sound of the iconic Walter Gross/Jack Lawrence classic ballad, "Tenderly", blown by black jazz man Joe Thomas,[*] with The Rhoda Scott Trio, wafted its way through the din and camouflage of cigarette smoke to my young and receptive ears.

How fitting and prescient, then, that the very first jazz album I subsequently acquired and listened to, *Exodus to Jazz*, by the tenor saxman, Eddie Harris, was to become for me like the Biblical Exodus story, the symbolic pathway to my own freedom of creative expression.

Many years later, remembering the choices, conflicts and all those rivers that we think we ought to have traveled to assuage our parents' fears for our destiny, it was easy to recall the kind eyes of my mother's father—my grandfather, my *zayde*—a sturdy baker who upon hearing those first alto sax notes which issued forth like his yeast with the promise of fulfillment, remarked exuberantly in his broken English, ***"Harrison, this is for YOU, to play the saxophone!"***

---

[*] Joseph Vankert Thomas (June 19,1909-August 3,1986) was an American jazz tenor saxophonist and vocalist. Among his many musical accomplishments, Thomas played with Jimmie Lunceford's band from 1933 until the leader's death in 1947, often soloing and occasionally singing.

Conversations

CONTENTS

List of Illustrations

Tools of the Trade

FORWARD

To Influence the World
According to Jazz:
A Musician/Writer's Calling

As an impressionable teenager navigating the musical waters of the early 1960's in multi-cultural New Bedford, Massachusetts, I quickly gravitated to jazz; my instrument of choice was the tenor saxophone. Gradually, with the mastery of craft, my music's internal voice began to emerge. Though a young voice, it was one with an old soul and sensitive to those who had developed this music as a vehicle for their survival.

While an undergraduate at Boston's Berklee College of Music, I was introduced to the classic jazz ensemble. This format, along with continued exposure to jam sessions, became the crucible for melding personal expression with a positive group interaction, thus creating a working ideal for social intercourse. In jazz music's unique improvisational design, I discovered an opportunity to create a highly personal and gratifying language of self-expression. Embellished by the creative spirit and imagination of its individual players, jazz music soon conveyed to me a most compelling message: *Through this uniquely bred American cultural art form, greater communication and understanding between men and women everywhere is possible.*

In naming and defining the role Dr. Saxx plays in the story, I have come to realize that this mentor has been drawn from one and several people in my life—those rare teacher/human beings who impart invaluable lessons for living and expanding. Through a diligent and purposeful study of the craft of jazz music, I have been given the key to opening the door to living sensitively and completely. When Dr. Saxx makes an important address to Stormy Keys, it is as if each one of us who loves the music, whether we play it or merely listen to it, cannot help but be, like Stormy, challenged to keep the chain unbroken. Ours then becomes a genuine commitment to pass along this wondrous legacy of jazz music given us by the African Americans.

When the youths meet as young adults in The Bass Clef, implicit in this, Stormy's final encounter with his jazz musician friend Forest Tune, lies the universal hope that through the playing and ennobling of jazz music, better communication among all persons, regardless of race, creed, color or gender may yet be advanced. In a world where all men and women can be brothers and sisters, there is no end to the possibilities!

I am passionate about jazz. I respect its roots and am committed to its future. It is my responsibility, I believe, to articulate this music's humanistic potential. In the hearts and minds of succeeding generations, jazz music's improvisational language can become both a tool for awakening self-discovery, and a model for learning how to live with one another, cooperatively and compassionately.

Harrison R. Goldberg
Gualala, California

Full Circle

PREFACE

Introducing *Once Upon a Tune*

Fasten your seatbelts and keep your hands inside the ride! You'll need to be anchored when you blast off on a syncopated, lyrical percussive journey in:

"Once Upon a Tune" by Harrison Goldberg.

Harrison cleverly captures the quest of most aspiring musicians who endeavor to find their sound, which is really his or her own voice. They strive to hear it, be associated with it and for it to become their unique expression. They seek to find that right combination of notes and perfectly arrange them. This is a life-long pursuit.

The story is more than a fast train that harkens you back to a time of golden music, with a Count, a Duke, a Queen and a plethora of newcomers trying to make the cut. At its heart, it's a story of friendship between two young men from two different worlds. A friendship cultivated through time, but not eroded by it. Yeah, a one in a million friendship that transcends space, time, history, race and gender. What more could I say? It's a friendship approved by our creator, the definition of agape love. It's a story of hope and love for the music and it pays homage to those players that paved the way, like Dr. Saxx.

Travel back to Harlem during The Golden Age of Modern Music. A truly fascinating journey.

Congratulations my brother. You found your voice. Thank you for that true love. Toast to our Berklee days.

Jimmy Kingsby
Saxophonist
Berklee College of Music
Class of 1978

In this remarkable book, Harrison Goldberg, storyteller, poet, artist and tenor saxophonist, tells a story of passion, perseverance and magical realism. I personally experience Harrison's music as thrilling, a physical experience transcending mere sound and creating an alternative reality. To hear his music is to be fully alive. It is a privilege to review this excellent book in which aspiring musicians will find inspiration and a deeper understanding of music and self.

Harrison is a gifted writer who has described an odyssey of passion and evolving faith in oneself. His use of magical realism throughout the story is reminiscent of the pioneering works of Garcia Marquez, Rushdie, Kafka and Morrison. Magic begins when the main character, Stormy Keys, finds the tenor saxophone in a music store that will shape his talent and provoke his journey. With a mermaid engraved on its bell, whiffs of sea air and the wetness of sea on his skin, Stormy and the reader are transported into a world where the senses are heightened by mysterious, sensual images; where anything can happen. Perhaps it is the siren of this Mermaid called Jazz that opened his mind to unheard of possibilities.

The journey begins through the voice of Forest Tune, a young African American man and friend of our main character, Stormy Keys. As narrator, Forest speaks with an authentic voice, one that represents the African American roots of jazz, his youth and his desires.

These friends are conflicted by their parents' opposition to their desires to visit Harlem and try out their interests in jazz. Will they be able to deal with the troubles to come? Will it be worth it? Their doubts are soothed by hundreds of phantom black and white birds in flight. Was this a sign that their dreams could come true? The spectacle gives them confidence to proceed.

They persevere. When at last the boys are given an opportunity to perform, Stormy couldn't find the melody, that "sweet music" borrowed from Middle English. He couldn't find that string of chords. Humiliated and shamed, he leaves the club. Forest doesn't notice him leave, so our narrator is temporarily left behind. As a white youth in Harlem, Stormy felt like a stranger in a strange land. He was "lost at sea and floundered," Forest later reflects. But it was not the color of his skin, but his lack of soul that created the distance from the world he sought. There are no accidents, Stormy philosophized later.

Yet we do not lose Forest's voice, as he continues to tell us of the wanderings of the lone Stormy, desperate to make sense of his life. That very night, Stormy comes upon The Bass Clef club where he encountered the sound of an otherworldly tenor sax, a golden note floating from its bell. The player, an elderly saxophonist named Dr. Saxx had been alerted by Jazz, the mermaid, to watch out for Stormy Keys. He recognized him right off. "I am the African American voice of the saxophone," he told Stormy, "jazz music that celebrates the freedom and spontaneous creative expression of a race of people who refused to die in an alien land." Dr. Saxx had chosen Stormy and becomes his mentor, the voice he will hear in his heart. The guide he needed. He gave Stormy a golden reed that will travel with him always. If he works hard, he is told, he will find his soul through a higher power, a little help from The Living Spirit.

Stormy finds Forest and tells him the story, then disappears. Where was he? The odyssey continued. Was he wandering in the wilderness? Did he become his own narrator? The author of his own story as Dr. Saxx had suggested?

Nearly ten years later Stormy returns triumphant to The Bass Clef. Forest Tune and his colleagues are performing but missing the tenor sax. Without hesitation or invitation, Stormy joins the performers, his sax singing with a golden energy, transcending any jazz that the human ear had ever heard. He was now among the greats, no longer in the shadow of, but performing in the company of such jazz tenor saxophone titans as Coleman Hawkins, Ben Webster, Lester Young, Dexter Gordon, Sonny Rollins, and John Coltrane. Harrison's description of Stormy's performance is masterful.

Life comes full circle when learners become teachers and teachers become learners. And teachers and learners become leaders. The dance continues. Stormy and Forest shared their talents by teaching young musicians at schools and universities around the country while their own talents, working together as "The Brotherhood o' Man," deepened.

This story, *Once Upon A Tune: One Young Man's Quest to Become a Jazz Saxophonist,* captures the essence of magical realism, metaphor, sensuality, rich description and melodies of emotion. By highlighting actions that propelled this young man, we learned of his inner world and the influences of imagination. We also learned of the power and history of jazz and the sounds that have given us meaning of what it is to be fully human. Harrison Goldberg offers up a great gift to the biography of jazz and of self through one young man's quest.

Yet, there is more. This magnificent story is accompanied by original abstract sketchings, poetry, pertinent quotations and an index of jazz greats. Together, this is a blend of art forms designed to deepen communication and understandings.

Linda Lambert, Ed.D.
Author and professor emeritus
California State University, East Bay
linlambert@mcn.org

ONCE UPON A TUNE

One Young
Man's Quest
to Become
a Jazz
Saxophonist

Cirque

PROLOGUE

Prologue

Some Words to All You Seekers
of the Sound

Lately I've been ponderin' music in the key o' life, or maybe it's jus' life in the key o' music that I've been thinkin' 'bout. Well, whatever, let me pose a question, an' I promise I won't git too philosophical on ya. Do ya suppose it's possible ta REALLY play in tune or, for that matter, ta even stay in tune while the rest o' the world whirlin' 'round ya is slightly out o' tune? That's gotta be a tough one. I mean, geez, what wit' tryin' ta earn your bread an' keep an' all, it takes everythang a cat's got an' then some jus' ta keep it together these days.

Fact is, the only real defense ya got in a world that's forever off key is ta keep both ears tuned ta that bright an' hopeful melody, ya know. If you're anythang like me, Forest Tune, you've probably had it in your head all along, at least as far back as when you was a kid. 'Course in my case, comin' from a family that jus' so happened ta be called "Tune," I can't evah remember bein' wit'out it. I mean, man, I had my tune wit' me right from the git-go. Now how 'bout that?

Seriously, the real truth o' the matter is that it ain't always gonna be an easy thing ta do—keepin' your ear on your song, your eye on the prize. For whatever reason, an' Lord knows there ain't no shortage of 'em, a man often gits sidetracked, waylaid, or else jus' plain distracted from his mission. I can tell ya it happens all the time, even ta the best o' us, an' usually when a cat is least expectin' it. Wit' so much diff'rent music comin' at 'im from all directions—an' some o' it mighty tantalizin' if I can say so myself—it's easy ta see why one day a fella jus' up an' leaves his own melody unsung by the side o' the road. An' then, wit' loads o' passion like it was his very own, the cat takes ta singin' an' playin' somebody else's song—doesn't even matter if it's good o' bad. 'Course by then, he's probably got blinders on an' sees an' hears only what he wants ta anyway.

Funny thang though, 'bout the time all this starts happenin', the dude finds it's 'specially hip ta play outside, I mean, now that he's driftin' away from his familiar turf, he starts takin' some liberties wit' the changes—cats be doin' it all the time. Some of 'em, though, can git so far out there that they need a road map or a rhythm section rescue party jus' ta help 'em git back home.

Still, after everythang's been said an' done, I'm sure most o' 'em would agree—if they hadna taken them chances, they wouldna known they'd been in tune in the first place, that is, if there really is such a thang as bein' in tune. But one thang's for sure, by the time they finally hook up wit' their lost melody, the song they be singin' is all the richer for it. Kind o' makes sense, don't it?

I think what it all really boils down ta is self-discov'ry. It's 'bout findin' that unique an' special voice that's livin' inside each an' every one o' us an' then expressin' it, no matter where an' how far out the journey takes ya. An' in case ya don't believe me, jus' stick 'round for the ride. You're gonna find that this is one trip that'll take a lifetime, ya'll see!

Forest Tune
Harlem, New York
July 4, 1980

Strange Fruit

SOMEPLACE, Nowhere

SOMEPLACE, Nowhere

I think playing the saxophone is
what I'm supposed to be doing on this planet.
It's the best way I know
that I can make the largest number of people happy
and get for myself
the largest amount of happiness.

~ Joe Henderson

Good evenin' an' welcome ta The Bass Clef…Thank you, thank you, yeah, brothers an' sisters, your applause is sweet. Oh yehh—we certainly thank y'all. Say, I see an awful lot o' familiar faces out there, but in case this here's your first vist ta The Clef, I'll let you in on a little secret. You might not be realizin' it jus' yet, but by the time ya'll be leavin' here, ya'll know you've been ta the core o' the Big Apple hitself. I'm talkin' ta ya 'bout nothin' less than Harlem, USA, though 'fore you can git down ta the real sweet fruit we be offerin', ya woulda had ta peel off, layer-by-sticky-layer, all that uptown-downtown-shiny-red-waxy-surface stuff. Man, ain't this town some kind o' tinsel circus? I hope ta tell ya!! Everybody's got their scam, always tryin' ta sell ya somethang. But brothers an' sisters, I gotta take my hat off ta yas. You wasn't buyin' the hype. Ya knew where you was headin'.

Tonight while y'all be down here soakin' up the sounds we be dishin' ya, there'll still be a lot o' hungry cats roamin' 'round town who'll never git the chance ta connect. Sure they might catch some elevator muzak comin' an' goin' but when it comes ta down-home-real-an'-honest-ta-goodness jazz, take it from me, Forest Tune, they're gonna come up short. Believe me when I tell ya—ain't nothin' soul satisfyin' in the watered-down musical diet some o' these folks be preparin' ta sample.

Even the highbrow "queezeen" they're fixin' ta scarf ain't gonna fill 'em up. 'Fore long, them bellies be rumblin' again. 'Course, jus' in case ya haven't already caught a whiff o' our ribs an' chicken a-slow simmerin', you're in for a treat. Then you'll surely be talkin', tellin' everybody from here ta Frisco that not only have ya heard the best jazz, but you've eaten the best barbecue in town an' that's no lyin.' At The Bass Clef we surely be cookin' an' wailin', wailin' an'-a-cookin'!

So without further delay, me an' the band we're gonna blast off so's ta give ya a taste o' what's in store for ya tonite—though first if ya don't mind, I'm goin' ta hook up wit' my bass—she don't partic'larly like bein' separated from me too long. Still, ya know what *they* say—whoever *they* are—absence makes the heart grow fonder. Well, let's jus' see if it works. Ahh...now that's more like it!! Jus' listen ta them strings shudderin'. Man, is she ever purrin' again. OK, ya cats ready?...Good!!...Then here's an original thang comin' at ya from yours truly, Forest Tune. We call this one "Brother o' the Treble," an' if ya already checked out the marquee on your way in tonight, then ya know that we be called, Brothers o' the Treble. OK, guys, let's do it!!!!...1, 2...1, 2, 3, 4...

...Yeah, your applause is surely sweet!... Hey, what'd I tell ya!! You're a hip crowd an' ya got big ears...Oh yehh!!...Thank ya... Now I know y'all specifically came down here tonite ta hear some tunes, an' don'cha worry, we're not 'bout ta disappoint ya. First, though, I got somethang else cookin' an' I invite y'all ta give a listen. This jazz music's been the better 'cause o' it. An' the sooner I git this story told, the sooner the road'll bring us back ta the sounds y'all came listenin' for.

An ol' piana man by the name o' T.C. Brown once told me, "There's only 88 keys on the piana, but deep down inside each an' every one o' them ivories, there's more than a million diff'rent ways for a fella ta reach out an' touch heaven's gate, if only for an instant. 'Course that fella still has ta want it badly enough wit' all his heart 'n soul, but even then there can be no guarantee. Top o' all that, he's gotta be plumb lucky, too. I mean the trick is ta get an invite from the Maestro himself, ya know, that cat o' all cats who controls the heavenly strings upstairs. Now there's the kicker!" Today I'm sure there'd be a lot o' cats who'd tell ya that jus' findin' the time ta sit down 'fore the piana would be heaven enough, never mind if they ever got the chance ta play one lonely note. You can imagine jus' how they'd feel if they was ever ta git their hands on all 88 o' them ivories. Nothin' shy o' pure ecstasy, ya can be sure!

Ta the fellow I'm fixin' ta tell y'all about, there never really was any diff'rence 'tween heaven an' music. Ta him, they was one an' the same. From the git, long as this cat was playin' his saxophone, or even listenin' ta jazz music, he was truly shinin' in that land o' glory, never mind jus' touchin' them pearly gates. Brothers an' sisters, let me tell ya—he was all the way in there!!!

Now don'cha be lookin' up here on this stage 'cause you ain't likely ta see the dude, not tonight nor, for that matter, anytime soon. Truth is it's been over ten years, maybe more, since I seen 'im, not since we was kids, an' Lordy only knows where he's at. An' that's too bad, 'specially since tonite we happen ta be runnin' wit'out our tenor sax man; there wasn't even time enough 'fore the gig ta cover for 'im. So in the end, we opted ta go it as a trio. Ya know—do the piana, bass, an' drums thang. Sometimes ya do what ya gotta do! It's as simple as that. In this business, not jus' anyone'll do. Sure, a cat's gotta have a ton o' chops ta hang but that's only one part o' it. You can't fool the audience, 'specially one wit' big ears like yas. No sirreeee! If there ain't no chemistry happenin' up here 'tween us, y'all be better off stayin' home an' cozyin' up ta your stereo. You'd probably git more pleasure from it.

Tonite on my way over ta the gig it was chemistry, yeh. I guess that's what started me thinkin' 'bout the kid. Sure, we could probably use someone jus' like 'im ta mix things up. By now, if he's still playin', which I don't doubt for an instant, I suspect wherever he's at he's gotta be some kind o' monster player. 'Course if all these years he's stayed sensitive ta the music comin' from the cats 'round him, then those chops would really add up ta somethang. But let me tell ya what I remember 'bout him that's still so fresh an' wonderful in my mind. All that other stuff—that's nothin' but conjecture, stuff ta dream on, an' that's a whole other ball game.

If ever ya could jus' look at a person an' instantly match 'em up ta a particular musical instrument, then this cat, a tall, skinny, freckled-face white kid, was surely born ta blow that tenor sax. In his huge hands, he'd make a nest for the great golden bird o' a horn that roosted there much o' the day an' even on inta his dreams at night.

Anytime he'd breathe life inta this sax, the bird would suddenly flutter its wings, an' wit' one or more healthy squawks, in an instant it'd be off an' flyin', well, sort o'.

In the beginnin', that bird could hardly get off the ground. Ya see, the kid was havin' one helluva time tryin' ta get his chops. Still, he declared he was gonna stay wit' it, no matter how long it took. He jus' knew that the song inside the golden bird had ta be a beautiful one an' once he found it, he'd set that bird free. An' that's when folks would surely start listenin' ta 'im, maybe even begin ta fall in love wit' his sound.

Say, I almost forgot ta tell ya his name, too busy ramblin' an' riffin'…Stormy Keys…yeah…Stormy Keys…. how 'bout that for a moniker? Man, it sure fitted him to a "T," 'specially the first part, the "Stormy." The cat was forever fightin' wit' his folks on account o' them not lettin' 'im git over ta Harlem ta dig the jazz scene. An' then there's the second part, the family name o' Keys—well, that jus' mighta been his destiny. I mean, nothang's ever written in stone, but maybe if he pushes down hard an' long enough on them sax keys, the cat'll finally come ta hear his own unique voice. Hey, he might even be lucky enough ta recognize it when, one day on its own accord, it comes pourin' out o' his horn.

Now 'bout that horn—no sense tryin' ta separate Stormy from it 'cause you ain't gonna really know 'im 'til you know somethang 'bout his axe. An' that's gonna be harder than ya think. I swear I've never seen another one like it before or since he first showed it ta me, an' how in the world he ever managed ta come by it—that's still a mystery ta me.

Says he was passin' some pawnshop way out on Broadway, when he gets this feelin', you know, like maybe he oughta go in an' check the place out. But it was really a much stronger feelin' than that. It was almost like he starts hearin' a voice inside his head coaxin' 'im ta go inside. That voice musta been really hard ta resist 'cause next thang Stormy knows, he's standin' in the shop. Ten minutes later he's walkin' out wit' the horn. It happened as quick as that. Still, he had some cash on 'im an' from the git go he had this notion ta get 'im a tenor saxophone.

So let me back up a piece ta that pawn shop. Yehh, I'm sure you've seen one o' 'em places, maybe even been in one or two o' 'em before. They all look alike ta me. But in case you haven't seen one, the kinda shop I'm talkin' 'bout is jus' bustin' out at the seams wit' instruments for makin' music. They got loads o' other stuff too. Since the beginning o' time, or so it seems, cats down on their luck be pawnin' away a vital piece o' their dreams in one o' these places; anythang for some quick cash. Some o' 'em are sure ta tell ya jus' for the sake o' talkin' an' convincin' themselfs otherwise, "Don't worry, I still got my ticket. 'Fore long I'll be back ta get my axe." But the real truth o' the matter is, an' jus' ask the cats who run these places, few of 'em really ever do. Most of 'em jus' ain't lucky enough that way. But in case you're fixin' ta get started on your own musical dream where somebody else's left off, you couldna picked a better place than a pawn shop. So go ahead. Here's a sample o' what you're likely ta find:

The musical stuff. It comes in all shapes an' sizes, jus' 'bout every color too. All you gonna need is a little cash an' then some chops. But don't worry 'bout your chops, that'll come later. Right now all ya wanna do is concentrate your energies on findin' ya that special axe. Cat I knew that made instruments had 'im a theory 'bout that—said he wished he'd taken pictures o' all his customers wit' the instruments they'd bought. He believed people really tended ta buy instruments that looked like 'em. It's really comical.

For now let's start wit' the clarinets an' flutes, or else maybe you'd like ta try a piccolo or a fife; they got 'em, I swear. Perhaps it's the trumpets that'll catch your fancy, or a Flugelhorn. There's even a French horn, some bugles, cornets, trombones, an' an old broken-down tuba that musta seen service wit' John Phillip Souza 'imself. Yeahh...if that's what ya want, you're sure ta find 'em. There are strings too, like violins an' violas, cellos, bass fiddles, guitars, banjos, ukuleles. There are drums, congas, bongos, bright red accordions, an' a glass case full o' harmonicas—instruments for everybody's tastes. Now you're probably wonderin' 'bout the saxophones. Well, the timin' is right 'cause I was jus' gettin' 'round ta tellin' ya 'bout 'em. After all, that's the only thang was on Stormy's mind the day he walked inta this pawn shop on Broadway.

Once inside, it didn't take Stormy long ta find the saxes. "Had ta be at least three dozen o' 'em," he said. There was the altos, tenors, an' sopranos, straight ones an' curved ones, a sopranino, an' finally a couple o' those big band war horses, the baritones. Some o' the saxes was silver-plated an' others gold. O' these, there was the really shiny ones an' right away they caught Stormy's eye. Then there was others sorta on the fringe, if ya know what I mean, wit' jus' the usual ding here an' there but otherwise in good workin' condition.

Well, these horns was all hangin' from hooks upside down along a side aisle an' as Stormy's walkin' an' checkin' 'em all out, he suddenly gits this weird feelin' as if someone or somethang was talkin' ta 'im sorta faint-like from over his left shoulder. Seemed that whoever or whatever it was, it was whisperin' ta 'im, an' he said he could even feel their hot breath blowin' in his ear. Said it made what little hair he had on the back o' his neck stand straight up. There was somethang else too. Along wit' the whisperin', Stormy says he began ta imagine 'imself down by the seashore, the invitin' smell o' a Cape Cod summer-sea-salt air, the kind that he used ta dream 'bout—though he'd never actually been there—beginnin' ta fill his nostrils. For a moment he closed his eyes an' coulda sworn he was hearin' the *G-O-N-G G-O-N-G* from what coulda been a buoy out at sea warnin' ships 'gainst the peril o' approachin' rocks. Then he thinks he saw a real ship, its fog horn blastin', come right out o' his daydream, passin' dangerously close ta those rocks 'fore disappearin' inta the mist. An' that's 'bout the time Stormy opened his eyes. Somethang made 'im put his hand on the back o' his neck. He didn't know why, but the skin back there was all wet an' when he tasted his hand, it filled his mouth wit' the salt o' the sea. Pretty strange, huh?

Ya can imagine what Stormy musta been thinkin'. "I only came in here ta find a sax an' now I must be losin' my mind. What in the world's goin' on anyway?" At first he thinks the whisperin' surely's gotta belong ta one o' the store's two clerks. He'd first noticed 'em when he walked in but when he turned 'round he sees both of 'em wit' the gray aprons an' plastic visors, busy showin' jewelry ta customers at a lighted display case along the store's rear wall, some distance away. They hardly seemed ta notice 'im.

An' that's when once again Stormy says he starts hearin' the voice, only this time it's real clear an' louder an' he can identify it as a female voice, sweet an' tantalizin', too. "Look now over your left shoulder," the voice was sayin'. "I'm on the bell o' the sax closest ta ya. Why don't ya reach up an' touch me. I won't bite ya."

An' that's just what Stormy does 'cause at this point it's almost like the voice was controllin' his every action; it was like that feelin' he'd first had when he was passin' the shop. He couldna resisted even if he'd wanted ta. Next thang he knows, he's holdin' what's gotta be the most ancient-lookin' tenor saxophone he'd ever seen, an' certainly the oldest sax in the place. It was soft an' smooth ta the touch an' glowin' the color o' warm honey, yes it was. Turnin' it 'round in his hand so that the bell's facin' 'im, he notices it has a curious engravin'—a mermaid in the sea in front o' a tropical island. An' there was even a sailin' ship passin' by in the distance.*

Suddenly Stormy starts puttin' it all together, the strange voice callin' out ta 'im, the smell o' the sea, an' even the foghorn blast o' the ship he'd imagined hearin' moments before. "Somethang doesn't seem ta be addin' up or maybe I'm jus' plain missin' the boat. Is it really her voice, this mermaid lady on the bell that I've been hearin? No, my mind must be playin' more tricks on me," he finally decides, an' he's 'bout ta hang up the old sax in exchange for a real shiny one he'd been eyein' earlier when all o' a sudden he says he actually sees this mermaid on the bell turn her head completely 'round so she's now facin' 'im eyeball to eyeball.

That's when she opens her mouth an' says in a real sweet voice (an' would ya believe she even knew his name), "Stormy, I'm called Jazz, the mermaid from the Sea of Time in The Land called Song, and I'm happy that you've made the right choice. Now, know that an exciting musical journey awaits you! Clearly my horn was meant for you, and one day, you're gonna find that this saxophone carries your life's own beautiful melody within it."

An' that was the beginnin' o' some strange things. As soon as

---

* The inspiration for "Jazz," the mermaid, came from a famous vintage series Conn M saxophone that was produced by the Conn Company from 1931-1969. These horns, commonly referred to as 'Naked Lady' models, sported an engraving of a naked lady on the bell. However, it is only considered a 'Naked Lady' if it has the naked lady engraving, which is merely the bust of a woman inside a pentagon surrounded by an Art Deco design. The Conn M horns were played by the likes of alto saxophonists Charlie Parker and Benny Carter, tenor saxophonists Dexter Gordon and Lester Young, and baritone saxophonists Gerry Mulligan and Harry Carney.

Stormy told the clerk he wanted to buy the old tenor, though he never said nothin' 'bout what he'd seen, heard or even smelled-that was his secret-the clerk turns ta 'im an' says, half mutterin' ta 'imself at the same time:

"Funny, for the life o' me, I can't seem ta place this one, an' I thought for sure that I'd got 'em all on the last inventory ...an' come ta think of it, this one doesn't even have a price tag. Kid, I wouldn't know what ta charge ya for it. This is pretty odd!" Hey Max!" he's shoutin' ta his fellow clerk, "ya evah seen this tenor before?"

After a few moments, Max, who was finishin' up wit' a customer, comes over, picks up the horn an' slowly starts turnin' it 'round in his hands. The whole time he's doin' the turnin', he's shakin' his head an' mutterin' ta 'imself jus' like the first clerk was.

"No, can't say I ever have," he finally says. "This one's a complete mystery ta me. I've gotta tell ya—and I've been in this business for over twenty-five years—that I've never laid eyes on its likes before. But hey now, wait a minute," an' he turns ta the first clerk an' says, "Ya know, Leo, we still gotta have some kind o' record o' it in our register. Let me look it up."

After a few more minutes, Max, scratchin' his head, turns ta Stormy an' says: "Incredible, I still can't believe my eyes. There's absolutely no record o' this sax at all...and not even a case to go with it! Still, it's clean enough an' the pads an' springs all look ta be in remarkable condition, 'specially considerin' it's age, though I really can't accurately judge that. Strange...wit' the exception o' this curious engravin', there's not even a serial number on it. Now that's bizarre...just goes ta show ya we're not perfect in this business. Guess this is that one in a million that somehow managed to slip through the cracks. ...Oh well!"

Then this first clerk, the one called Leo, turns to Stormy an' asks 'im, "So, it's this old woman you got your heart set on, huh kid? Well I see she even has herself a couple o' good dents down below the bell. Look kid, since I got no record o' it, I'll let you have it for $400. Furthermore, ta show you how good a sport I am, I'll even throw in a case; I think we can find a neck strap too, a decent mouthpiece with cap 'n' ligature, an' a box o' reeds. That oughta get ya rolling. What do ya say?"

Stormy couldna have been happier an' he could hardly contain 'imself, he was so excited. Quickly, an' before the clerk could change his mind, Stormy put his cash down on the counter. Surprise o' all surprises it was exactly $400, all the money he'd managed ta save on his last summer's job. An' the last thang he remembered hearin' the clerk say before he hit the street was, "Well, kid, looks like ya just got youself a deal. Good luck!"

An' that's how Stormy got 'im that tenor sax. While most o' the other kids at our school was sportin' brand spankin' new axes their parents had bought 'em, Stormy had an old horn wit' that lady o' the sea on it. He couldna cared less what the other kids thought. Nothin' seemed ta bother 'im, even when the other kids took ta teasin' 'im an' laughin' at his horn, callin' it "an old clunker that shoulda been put ta pasture a long time ago," or else they'd say, "it was nothin' but a honey-combed pea shooter," or "some relic that was washed up from the sea."

No, none o' that ever mattered ta Stormy. Somehow he knew, 'cause o' the mermaid on the bell, this had ta be the most special horn o' all. So he'd let 'em all laugh. One day soon he knew he'd get his chance ta show 'em. After all, the mermaid had actually talked to 'im 'bout an excitin' musical journey he was gonna take an' he had no reason not ta believe her. The only question he had was, "When would it begin?"

That's when I stepped inta the picture. Things had their own way o' takin' off from there. Ya know, I can remember as plain as day the first time Stormy an' me met. It was on the subway, both o' us was carryin' our music cases, me wit' the oversized violin suitcase, Stormy wit' his tenor sax. The cat had a grin big enough ta have its own suitcase. Headin' ta school ta take some music classes, we knew, right from the moment that train started movin', that we was destined ta become runnin' mates, the best o' buddies. We was teenagers back then. The surprise o' all surprises came when we found we even lived on the same block, 'though it was a mighty big block; I lived way down at the lower end o' it. Come ta think o' it, I jus' mighta been the only black kid in Flushing Meadows, Queens, or at that time at least, the only one in our school who played the string bass. But it was pure love for jazz music we had in common, that's for sure.

Through our record albums, Stormy an' me both found an' shared an excitin' new world. Wit' what little money we collected from a series o' after school jobs, as well as during our summer vacations, we each managed ta put together, if I must say so myself, a pretty impressive an' sizeable record collection o' our favorite jazz artists.

Jus' like the famous baseball players o' our day, these jazz cats were our heroes, plain an' simple. An' certainly there was no denyin', that like the ball players, these jazzers also had this special aura 'bout 'em. During those days, I think that if anyone on the street had overheard us talkin' an' didn't know the foggiest thang 'bout jazz music, they'd probably sworn we was talkin' 'bout baseball players 'stead o' musicians. An' that's really 'cause the names o' the most popular jazz players an' the instruments an' bands they played wit' wasn't much diff'rent from knowin'—an' even talkin' 'bout— who was playin' each position for, say, a team like the New York Yankees. An' it sounded the same too, 'specially when you got ta runnin' the name o' this or that jazz giant along wit' a recountin' o' some fabulous exploit where the cat gave the fans somethang extraordinary ta remember 'bout his band's performance. 'Member that time in Newport, Rhode Island, when Paul Gonsalves, a tenor man wit' the Ellington band, brought the packed festival house ta its feet when he played, wit'out stoppin', 32 consecutive solo choruses—each one diff'rent an' more excitin' than the ones that came before? Wouldn't be any less powerful a reaction than if the cat had hit a string o' home runs. But in the end, even after the music, it came down ta their nicknames, an' those names told volumes of stories 'bout the music. Jus' ta hear 'em mentioned, an' even a couple o' female vocalists, ya could swear ya was at a ballpark, an' I'm not talkin' 'bout sandlot either. This here's the majors an' these were the major players!!

We even had us this wild theory 'bout jazz an' baseball, somethang that only happened on a certain night when the moon was full, blood red, an' hangin' in jus' the right spot over Shea Stadium.* When ya got all those combinations o' things workin' together for ya, then here's what would happen. 'Course all the time you'd be leadin' up ta it real slow ta get the

---

* See the spoken-word piece in the After Hours section, page 57: *Imagine if Jazz Were Like Baseball: Homage to the Greats.*

right effect. First, the park lights gotta go out, an' this is long after the last spectator, along wit' the coaches, players, umpires, vendors an' police have gone home. Suddenly, an' I might add, mysteriously, the park lights come on again. Then from literally nowhere, all these jazz players, scores o' 'em together—both the livin' an' the dead—start appearin' an' gatherin' behind home plate. They're carryin' their instrument cases wit' 'em but the vocalists, male and female, are carryin' old- fashioned radio microphones.

It's enough ta give ya the creeps. I mean this is not your usual happenin' like a jam at Small's Paradise. This here's behind home plate at Shea Stadium, in the wee hours, an' these cats, totin' their axes and not baseball bats, are stylin' in zoot suits and alligator shoes, with some even sportin' fedoras. The ladies, too, are high steppin' an' decked out in colorful, slinky dresses wit' feather boas an' pearls. Next thang ya know, they'll each have a go at their version o' the Great American game. Can ya dig, say, seein' the likes o' Satchmo wit' his horn, swingin' ta a mean fast ball. Well, that's what I'm talkin' 'bout here so are ya wit' me, 'cause here's the rest o' the scenario Stormy an' me cooked up, so check it out!

Its bases loaded an' top o' the ninth wit' the score all tied up 3 to 3 'tween these two teams. The jazz players could have been called the Catzanjammers, though I can't recall the name we gave 'em. They were up at bat 'gainst some all-star crusher lot, the Out o' Tuners. Can't ya see it? Some kinda showdown comin' an' this cocky southpaw pitcher wit' chew in his jaw has no idea what's in store for 'im. He's probably thinkin' ta 'imself, "Who do these cats think they are, anyway? A bunch o' sorry-lookin' musicians posin' as ball players? Hell, I've never even heard o' any o' 'em. Ya jus' watch me knock 'em out o' the batter's box. Piece o' cake! It's only a matter o' time before I git my glory; ya'll see soon enough!"

But ya know that's gotta be no mean feat, 'specially considerin' he be facin' the likes o' "Satchmo," "Prez," "Frog," an' maybe even a gal called "Lady Day." Now add "Bird," "Diz," "Dex," "Newk," "Miles," an' "Bix" an' ya know he definitely got his work cut out for 'im. But hold on 'cause I'm not through yet. In the dugout we still got "Hamp," "Lucky," "Shorty," "Pee-Wee," an' "Flip," wit' even more heavy hitters on deck. How 'bout Cannonball, the "Duke," the "Count," "Trane," "Monk," "Bunk," "Slam," an' a drummer called "Stix." Now that's what I call a pretty impressive line-up, wouldn't ya say? Surely this pitcher better be packin' his bags after they finish 'im up, an' baby I ain't lyin'. If ya know their music, then ya know this pitcher's end is surely comin'!

Ta us, jus' 'bout every time one o' these jazz cats picked up his axe, he'd hit home runs. It wouldn't matter how fast the pitcher be wailin' 'em; he'd still hit 'em way, way out o' the park. Only 'stead of baseballs he be lettin' fly these big, crisp, rich an' full musical notes, an' beltin' 'em way off inta outa space. An' ya can trust me when I tell ya, there ain't an outfielder on this planet gonna bring those notes down once they take ta flyin'. For one thang, there ain't no outfielder tall enough gonna git his glove up that high. Whoowee! Man, now we're really gittin' inta some *astronome!* An' if y'all be kind enough ta allow me a brief moment on that subject 'fore goin' on, I'd surely 'preciate it.

Do ya evah wonder 'bout the stars shinin' up there, perhaps billions of 'em? Well, we would reckon that they got brighter an' brighter each an' every time one o' 'em fat notes finally reached 'em. So what ya really be seein' when ya look overhead inta a night sky is jazz music turned inta pure golden light. That's gotta be some bright echo o' love an' beauty. Now since the stars are supposed ta be planets, an' jus' in case they got people, or else some other form o' bein' livin' on 'em, by now they'd have ta be pretty special. I mean, jus' think 'bout all those heartfelt notes the cats down here be dishin' 'em.

Yet even wit' all the listenin' we did, it wasn't until we had actually gone over ta Harlem that we would at last find the source that brought our record albums ta life. We called it "Our River" an' as time passed, this river o' ours became bigger than life hitself. Ta think that one day we might even git ta go ta the place where for us the jazz waters truly started flowin' was becomin' more an' more a possibility.

Actually, there was two other rivers, smaller ones but still no less important. They flowed directly from our river as did anythang at all connected wit' the music we loved. While I immediately picked up on the rhythm thang, Stormy, being a sax player, was drawn ta the melody. Do ya know that he used ta say the melody was like a beautiful princess, can ya imagine that? An' so, right then an' there he made up his mind ta follow her, even ta the ends o' the earth if he had ta. There really was no tellin' where she'd eventually lead 'im. Hopefully though, it wouldn't be astray—haaa, haa!!...Well, ya gotta know these sax players, they're an entirely diff'rent breed o' cat, an' believe me when I tell ya I know what I'm talkin' 'bout. I've gigged an' hung out wit' more than my share o' 'em.

There's one in particular really stands out in my mind though I never did git the chance ta meet 'im. O' course, it was Stormy who first told me 'bout 'im. The cat was diff'rent but in a special sort o' way. Anyway, that's Stormy's story an' a fantastic one, I might add. I'll never forget the chills I felt when he first shared it wit' me.

It was a sunny Sunday afternoon in late August when Stormy an' me finally decided ta go over ta Harlem. I mean jus' how many albums can ya sit at home listenin' ta, an' how long can ya go on talkin' 'bout somethang before there comes a time when ya gotta git up an' jus' do it, particularly when all your heroes are only a stone's throw away. Now, not tomorrow, was the time ta put our brave words inta action an' see how far they'd take us!!

Wit' me I always thought it would be easier, I mean, bein' a black kid an' all, an' 'specially wit' my folks comin' from Harlem too. Still, in the end, they nixed my goin' over there no matter how hard I'd plead my case for the music. Seems wit' me bein' their only child, they had this terrible fear that once I got ta Harlem, I'd fall in with the wrong crowd an' screw up my life forever.

So even after all that, I gotta tell ya I had me one helluva time climbin' down the fire escape, six flights in all, haulin' my string bass after me. Unless ya got a strong enough reason, an' a back ta match, I don't advise any of yas tryin' it. 'Course ya could rig youself a parachute an' float down. That'd be like a dream. Ya know there are some dreams that refuse ta wait for ya ta attend ta 'em. They creep inta ya at all hours o' the day an' prod an' prod until ya finally get their message. An' that's the day when you're ready ta bring 'em singin' ta life. Mine an' Stormy's was jus' that kind o' dream an' we was preparin' ta make it a reality no matter what the cost.

Because at the time it had made quite an impression on me, I can still remember clearly, even though it was more than ten years ago, Stormy tellin' me how he finally got up the nerve ta bolt from his apartment an' join me for the trip ta Harlem.

First, Stormy's mother says ta 'im, "There really should be no argument from ya, Stormy, and we've discussed this wit' ya for the very last time! Your father an' me feel very strongly that Harlem is nowhere for a boy like ya ta be, an' so you'd be foolish ta even think 'bout it any further. We forbid ya ta go, an' that's that!"

Then Stormy comes back wit', "But what 'bout the music? How am I ever going ta really learn how ta play jazz? Everyone knows you've gotta go ta the source if you really wanna learn this music!"

That's when Stormy's mother says, "Why don't ya jus' forget this silly notion ya have ta go ta Harlem? After all, ya have youself a record player. If ya go over ta Harlem, you'll surely git your horn stolen. I know it ain't a new one but still, ya had ta work an entire summer jus' ta be able ta afford ta buy it. If we had ta, we would be hard pressed ta help ya replace it. Ya know we work hard enough jus' ta make ends meet. Worse yet, you'll git in wit' the wrong crowd. I've heard that some pretty terrible things go on up there. Ya wanna play, fine, so why don'cha jus' wait until the high school marching band starts up in the fall. You'll certainly git all the music you'll need right there!"

Well, o' course all this jus' made Stormy real mad, so he goes straight ta his room. Still broodin,' he told me the first thang he does is turn on his record player. That's when he happens ta notice this record lyin' out o' its jacket. Turns out it's a real gem: the late great Coleman Hawkins, father o' the jazz tenor saxophone, an' his band, playin' an instrumental version o' the Edward Heyman, Johnny Green standard, *Out of Nowhere*.

For a while the music seems ta take Stormy out o' the doldrums. He even takes out his tenor an' starts jammin' wit' Coleman an' the guys. Then, that infernal subway goes by—it happens all the time 'round here jus' when you're diggin' on some great sounds—the needle on the machine up an' sticks, an' my man Stormy gets ta thinkin' 'bout what his mother said 'stead o' all the slick music comin' out o' the Hawk's horn. His own needle seemed ta be jus' plain stuck on that one word, "NOWHERE," an' it screamed in his head.

Then suddenly he gets this flash. He starts thinkin' 'bout what Dex said, ya know, the man 'imself, Dexter Gordon, a tenor giant in his own right. Somethang Dex once said on an album cover came ta Stormy right then an' there an' it went somethang like this, "It's important ta learn the words ta the song. They tell the whole story, what the writer had in his mind in the first place. Once ya know the words, you'll play 'em on your horn jus' the way they was meant ta be sung by a vocalist. Then, you'll be able ta say the music is truly your own. Remember, the key is in the lyrics!"

Well, for the life o' 'im, Stormy can't remember any words ta tunes, only the tunes themselves. But somehow the words from *Out of Nowhere* popped into his mind, an' then, over an' over he keeps repeatin' 'em, so as not ta forget, 'specially this part:

> "You came to me from out of nowhere,
> You took my heart
> and set it free.
> Wonderful dreams,
> wonderful schemes
> from nowhere..."

It seemed like them words was surely tryin' ta tell 'im somethang an' sure 'nough, they was, 'cause right then Stormy up an' says ta 'imself, "That's it, o' course, *Out of Nowhere*. I shoulda known it all along. It's Harlem, that's my *Nowhere*! And if it's really my *Nowhere*, then I should go there, 'cause at least it's *My **SOMEPLACE**, Nowhere*!" An' believe me, let me tell ya that nothang, nothang was gonna stop me an' that kid from goin' over ta Harlem that afternoon.

How could anythang possibly go wrong? I mean how could it—man, did we have it down!! Wasn't even a remote chance o' a slip-up. Since the day we agreed on where we was goin', we'd rehearsed the trip out loud over an' over an' over again, at least a dozen times or more an' no exaggeratin';'fore long we knew the route like the veins on the backs o' our hands. From Queens at Willets Point ya took the Flushing IRT at Times Square, then ya caught the A-train uptown ta Harlem an' got off at 135th Street. We even knew what ta do once we got there. It was that simple!

It was called *Squire's Place* at 2245 Seventh Avenue—between 132nd an' 133rd Streets—an' all the cats who could play, even as far away as Jersey knew 'bout it. "Hottest jam session in the Apple," they'd say. "All the action 'bout 4 PM an' goin' past midnight, ya can count on it! Anybody wit' their axe always welcome—chance ta play wit' the pros."

We'd even heard 'bout it from the brother we ran into on the street. Rim Shot was slick-headed, all tatted and muscular...an' he meant business...and his was the final word that convinced us! "So ya fellas wanna learn ta play jazz? Well, yas ain't never gonna learn nothang sittin' at home an' fantasizin'. Better git youselfs off ta *Squire's Place* in Harlem. Now there's a place can give ya your beginnin'!"

Seven days a week, an' in all kinds o' weather—which never seemed to bother 'im—the cat would set up his pearl-white-weather-beaten traps under an oilskin tarp he hung outside the subway tunnel we used on our way to and from school. An' anytime o' day we'd happen ta be passin' by, there'd be Rim Shot grinnin' an' workin' up a mighty sweat, showcasin' his burnin' stick attacks for spare change, an' sometimes if he was lucky, for a few stray bills. Top o' all that he be singin' the blues, or else playin' 'em wit' a tarnished old harmonica attached ta a metal frame hangin' 'round his neck. We figured if Rim Shot could hang tough in the streets for the music he loved, the least we could do was take his wise advice—we owed 'im that. So it was in the cards; we was destined ta go ta Harlem. It was jus' a matter o' time, an' there was no two ways 'bout it. The die was already cast!!

But when we finally hooked up where we'd said we would, by the entrance ta Flushing Meadows Corona Park, the thrill was gone. 'Stead o' glowin' over our new-found freedom an' the comin' adventure, we took ta leanin' 'gainst our cases an' starin' down at the ground. Not so much as a word passed 'tween us, though I'm sure Stormy had ta be thinkin' 'bout the same as me. Do I wanna do this? Is it really worth all the grief I'm gonna catch from my folks in the end? Do I need the hassles?

What was in store for us when our folks discovered us missin' now lay heavy on our bones; surely they'd put two an' two together. For two young bird-men supposedly settin' out on some important musical mission, we suddenly discovered our wings had been clipped.

An' funny thang, it was us who'd done the clippin'. Not exactly a healthy way ta begin flyin' inta our dreams, no sirreee!!

Well, after a while we got real tired of jus' starin' at the ground, so we picked up our axes an' walked a ways inta the park. Man I gotta tell ya that afternoon it sure was still, real still, an' awful hot an' muggy too! So here we was shufflin' along in a daze, sort o' like sleepwalkin' an' with all that heavy stuff goin' on in our heads, when we look up an' happen ta see the World's Fair Unisphere—like we almost could avoid it! Here it is, a gargantuan stainless steel globe, all 900,000 pounds of it, risin' twelve stories high in the air. Well, jus' as we was dead on it, suddenly out from the globe pours this tremendous mass o' black an' white birds, all wailin' an' jabberin' ta beat the band. There had ta be hundreds o' 'em, maybe even thousands, an' I'm not puttin' ya on. Wasn't long 'fore the sky was like a blue dish all salt an' peppered wit' 'em birds, an' still they kept comin' up from inside the globe.

I hope ta tell ya that this was no ordinary kind of thang, not on your life!! There are birds an' then there are birds. No, this coulda only been some kinda sign from the *Big Man* 'imself up in the *Big House* behind the sky doin' everythang he could ta catch our attention. An' catch it he sure did!! Right then an' there we jus' knew it had ta be his way o' sayin', **"This is your day—Go for it, Go, Go, GO!"** But for all we knew, it coulda been a dream, an' 'stead o' birds what we was really seein' was so many black an' white folks, flocks o' 'em together, sheddin' their earthly forms at the same time an' leavin' behind 'em all their cares an' the things that divided 'em. Yeahhh, there they was, no longer birds anymore wit' flutterin' feathers, but folks singin' an' celebratin', risin' up an' flyin' free ta some special place, a world where diff'rent dreams an' songs can live side by side. Man, it sure was a beautiful sight. An' then, in a flash they was gone, every last one o' 'em. Strange! It was as quick as that! An' so we was too, out o' the park as fast as we could go an' onta the subway.

Next thang we knew we was in Harlem, the late afternoon sun shinin' down on us, an' we're standin' outside Squire's Place in a line o' musicians an' wannabe's, a line that by that time was practically stretchin' halfway down the block. At last our dream had come true; we'd finally reached the source o' the river!! In lookin' back on it now, I think I know what mighta happened ta some o' those birds we'd seen in the park. For all we knew, they mighta changed inta that hopeful lookin' sea o' black an' white faces we was joinin' who carried their individual dreams inside 'em an' the means ta unlock those dreams in sax, trumpet, guitar, an' bass cases. Wit' our instruments, we was jus' two o' the many who hoped ta have their moment in the sun, sittin' in an' jammin' wit' the ace rhythm section o' Squire's Place's red-hot house band. We could hardly wait for the chance ta prove ourselves.

When that time came, we knew it wouldna matter a hill o' beans what color we was—black, white, yellow or tan. Each of us'd still have 'im the same opportunity ta blow a chorus or two, hey, maybe even get ta make it three or four if he was lucky enough. Long as ya truly loved the music an' had this burnin' desire ta play it, that's 'bout the only thang that'd count for real. We was bankin' on it!!

'Course we never stopped ta consider if what we was fixin' ta play would ever make any sense ta whoever'd be out there in the audience listenin'; we wasn't exactly thinkin' 'long those lines. Who knows though, maybe if we had, we mighta had second thoughts 'bout walkin' in as we was that day. But then again, we had no way o' knowin' beforehand that there was some cats inside who couldn't wait for the chance ta cut us wit' their axes, ya know, showin' us new bloods comin' up that they could out-play us, or take us down a peg or two. Sure, we'd all heard those war stories 'bout 'em before, but that's always the kind o' stuff that happens ta other dudes, never ta us.

Cats like this fancied themselves ta be the meanest, baddest jazz gunslingers in town, 'though ta look at most o' 'em, ya could plainly tell they hadn't been playin' the game too much longer than we had. More than likely, they was upstart sax an' trumpet players, an' some already had a couple o' fancy licks in a bunch o' keys already in their bag that they could run fast an' loud wit'. Else ya might come up 'gainst a piana or bass man, who, for no other reason than ta let ya know who was runnin' the show, would try ta waste ya from the git-go by settin' up a tempo he jus' knew would be impossible for ya ta follow. Then again, it might be your musical fate ta come up 'gainst a stick-trick—a dazzlin' drummer—some Mr. Flash-in-the-pan who couldn't find the beat for all the fireworks he be settin' off. Still, he'd make ya look ridiculous, sort o' like you was pantomimin' your axe 'stead o' really blowin' ta be heard over all that stuff he be dishin'. Man, I hope ta tell ya, when you're jus' startin' out, all o' that can really keep a cat from goin' on.

But I've come ta find out that every experience, 'specially these bad ones, will be useful for ya in some way later on. At the time, though, it sure seems ya got your work cut out for ya, an' then some, jus' ta find a way ta get through 'em. Then afterwards, it's all in how ya choose ta use 'em, ta really look at thangs, that's what's important. An' I guess if we're lucky ta live long enough, sooner or later we'll see that almost everythang has its own time an' reasons for happenin'. There ain't nothin' ya or I or anybody else can do ta change that! No sirreee! So ya might as well do like the boxin' man says—*just roll wit' the punches!!* You'll come out o' this ring better for it.

Now I don't exactly remember how long we'd been hangin' in that line. I jus' knew it had ta have been a good while 'cause the same hot dog vendor got our business three separate times when he made his pass up an' down the block, an' good thang too!! Wit' it bein' so hot an' our stomachs growlin' out o' tune, the lemonade an' dogs the cat was pushin' sure got us through.

Next thang we knew, we'd reached the front o' the building an' the door ta Squire's Place opened an' we was bein' ushered down some stairs by a big burly doorman who called 'imself, "Jock the Bouncer." Puffin' out his chest, he delivered what was probably his trademark schtik ta remind all us jazz wannabees jus' who was runnin' the show.

"I'm 'Jock the Bouncer, Keeper o' the Gate, the Cat who gets ta decide your Fate.' So ya wanna play jazz, that's what they all say...blow your horn, seize the day. But when you're too young ta stay, it's my job ta give ya the boot an' send ya on your way. I can put ya in the audience or up on that stage, or else toss ya in the gutter if trouble makin's your game. Who gits in, who goes out, that's my commission an' that's my clout!"

"I've seen it all from braggards ta brawl, in rain, sun an' sleet. While saxes an' drums be havin' their fun, you'll find me at the head o' the line an' always in the street. This bouncer's gig is full o' fights an' fisticuffs; seems there's never a bright moment in my life 'til a pretty face smiles at me. Always remember, when push comes ta shove, A Bouncer's Power, Don't Evah Doubt!"

'Course from the git-go, Jock knew we was under-age; it didn't take a genius ta figure that one out. He made us promise not ta touch a drink other than a Coke even if it was offered ta us. We figured it wasn't a difficult promise ta keep, 'specially considerin' he threatened ta break our legs if we didn't keep it, an' at last he finally let us in. I think he could see we'd come quite a ways in the heat luggin' all our gear an' he clearly felt sorry for us. As we passed inta the crowd at the club's entrance, we heard 'im shout over our shoulders, "Remember ta git your best licks in. Knock 'em dead; I'll be listenin' an' rootin' for yas!"

"Ya can count on it," Stormy an' me eagerly answered in unison as we entered—what to our surprise—turned out ta be a dark an' smoky windowless cellar club. No music was playin'; the band musta been on a break. Well, they're entitled ta one every once in a while, don'cha think? After all, it stands ta reason when ya be playin' that hard...

Well, before we could sit down, we got asked ta write our names in a big notebook 'long wit' the instruments we was fixin' ta play. We found out they usually did it this way at Squire's Place so anyone who came in ta jam wouldn't git passed over. Not a bad idea. An' most importantly, we learned that from this list o' players, the rhythm section could put together diff'rent combinations o' instruments. It made the music all the more interestin', like teamin' up a tenor wit' a trombone, an' then maybe even addin' a guitar ta give it a new twist. Shows ya all the possibilities—there's no end ta 'em. It's sort o' like cookin' up a dish by addin' all these exotic spices ta flavor it so it's extra special an' the crowd likes it too.

Chops, the cat who was handlin' that department was a musician 'imself—obviously a veteran o' hundreds o' these jam sessions. He told us, "Wit' all the musicians already sittin' in the house, it'll be some time 'fore the band will call ya up, but don't worry. Ya may be here all night, but you'll still git the chance ta play...and it might be sooner than later. Ya can see by this book tonight we got more than our share o' trumpet an' alto players but for some reason I only see a half dozen tenor players. Except for Truck, our regular bass man, you're it on the stand-up, kid, 'course first off we'll have ta see what ya can do. For now why don't yas take a load off an' make youselfs at home. Last time I looked I saw an empty table left o' the stage. Ya might wanna check it out an' chill 'til they call ya up."

We made our way along the crowded bar 'til we found that one empty table, set in a corner all by hitself near the stage; it was perfect an' mighta had our names on it, a good thang, too, 'cause there wasn't another one in the joint. Felt good ta sit again after hangin' so long in the street. I immediately leaned my bass 'gainst the wall an' Stormy slid his tenor case under the table. We had settled in for the long haul. Man, was it ever dark; we coulda been in a cave an' there was no way o' knowin' if it was still daylight outside. The only light was comin' from candles set into small glass bowls on each table, light which turned inta fireflies if ya looked back at the bar. There was two giant ceiling fans whirlin' overhead, people talkin' an' smokin', ice clinkin' in glasses, an' pretty waitresses rushin' past wit' loaded trays, ya know, the usual club scene. When we finally got our Cokes, the stage lights had gone up an' the band was takin' its place.

Stormy an' me once pictured that playin' in our first jazz jam session would be like participatin' in some special ritual...ya know, sorta like bein' at some magical campfire all glowin' with possibilities. We could jus' see it...it's a dark night wit' them bright stars starin' down, an' there we be, all huddled 'round this burnin' rhythm section...an' surrounded by a thick forest o' unseen eyes—the audience, o' course—peerin' in at ya. Then...suddenly from someplace way out there, a cool, cool wind comes blowin'. Soon the coals o' that rhythm section start glowin' an' out o' those flames, shadows o' trumpets, t-bones, an' saxes get ta jumpin', shoutin', an' story-tellin',...an' we're holdin' back the phantoms o' the night!!

Even before the band started playin', ya could tell right off that the brother sittin' in on the alto had an attitude. Maybe it was 'cause o' those shades he was wearin' or else the way he slouched 'gainst the piano wit' that cigarette danglin' from his lips that gave 'im away. But this kid, whose name they said was Bobby Blue, couldna been much older than me and Stormy and when he took ta his silver alto sax, from the git go he plain blew us all away!! The cat was burnin'...an' believe me when I tell ya that ev'ry note hit the bull's eye!!...the clean tone, the savvy o' his solos...I never heard 'im run out o' ideas...an' he never, an' I mean *never* ever played the same lick twice...an' then there was his speed—nobody could run notes faster. ...Too bad, years later I heard that this same kid with all the promise in the world had a tragic ending, but there's no need to get inta that now.

If you'd only let me, I could go on an' on 'cause this kid had it all!... On top o' that, the cat even knew when ta lay out an' give the piana man or bass man his due. You coulda sworn you was listenin' ta the man 'imself— Charlie "Yardbird" Parker. In fact, on several occasions, there was almost a note-for-note imitation o' "Bird" in the kid's solos...an' when he really got up ta speed, those seasoned veterans backin' 'im had real trouble keepin' up. A couple o' times, ya could tell the kid was goin' at it alone 'til the others caught up. Under the spotlights ya could even see those boys strainin', buckets o' sweat pourin' from 'em. But they was grinnin' at the same time, too. That kid really put the band through its paces wit' everythang from bop ta ballads. An' we wasn't the only ones impressed. You shoulda seen all those groupies hangin' near the stage checkin' out the kid. Wowweeee!!! Naturally the kid ate it all up, an' when he wasn't playin', he'd be struttin' 'round the stage posin' like some proud peacock showin' hitself off.

Listenin' ta the kid made us real hot ta play, but it would still be a while before we'd actually get ta sit in...then, right after the band comes back from its first break, the kid, who obviously was bein' given the chance ta run the Squire's Place show that afternoon, grabs the mic an' starts callin' cats wit' their axes up ta the stage, first one at a time, then groups o' 'em. While we waited patiently—as best as we could—for our turn, we sat an' listened an' man, did we ever get us an earful!

Over the next couple o' sets we heard the kid blowin' his best wit' some bones, some altos, a couple o' trumpets, a guitar player, a half dozen tenor players, an' even a cat on French horn—really cool. There was even a few female vocalists thrown inta the mix ta make thangs really interestin'. The kid really dug the singers, but over the long haul, we couldn't help noticin' that he could be partic'larly hard on some guys if he didn't dig what they was playin', or if there was some competitive thang goin' on.

Still, all that was nothang compared ta what happened ta Stormy when we finally got our own moment in the sun.

I'm almost sure o' it, though at first we could hardly believe it, that it was during the last set when we finally heard our names called. Well, praise the Lord!! It was 'bout time; at last it was true. We was now totin' our trusted pieces up ta the stage ta participate an' celebrate this thang called jazz. The deal was for me ta replace Truck, the band's regular stand-up bass man, while Stormy had 'imself the unenviable position of frontin' our group. The kid, meanwhile, had decided ta chill from the sidelines wit' a couple o' sisters, an' check us out.

It's been more than a few years, an' by now I figure I've played at least a thousand tunes. Now jus' 'cause my name's Forest Tune, don'cha go expectin' me ta remember the name o' this tune or that one that some piana man called out way back then. But that night, I jus' know the one we began wit' had ta have been some straight ahead jazz number wit' a killer tempo, a real tough one ta follow even if ya happen ta be a top notch jazz player.

We was jus' barely settled on stage when all o' a sudden the drummer, who obviously hadn't told anyone else but the piana player what tune we'd be playin', kicks off this wicked time wit' his sticks on the rim o' the snare: ...one, two...one, two, three, four...next thang I know we're off!!... but then I notice Stormy turned 'round in my direction, his horn danglin' from its neck strap, his face all screwed up wit' fear...an' he seemed ta be sayin', "What key are we in anyway?!! Oh no, I don't know this one!!" But what did I know, I'm no lip reader, an' besides, I had my own work cut out for me jus' ta hang wit' those rhythm cats pushin' me. I'll let ya in on a secret—I didn't know the head either. I guess I was lucky; wit' my big ears I was able ta fake my way in. So what did I do but turn away an' lose myself in my bass. By now Stormy was late comin' inta the head an' you can tell from what he's playin' that he doesn't know the tune from Adam...lost at sea an' flounderin'... that's where he was!!

But he wouldn't admit it, not ta 'imself, an' certainly never ta the band. That's jus' the way he was. After a while, ya couldn't even tell what tune we was playin' or, for that matter, what key we was in.

Still, that wasn't goin' ta stop Stormy Keys, no sireee!!!...Right out o' botchin' up the head, he starts ta solo: runnin' changes that won't let 'im get a handle on 'em, stompin' all over the stage, honkin' an' shovin' the bell o' his horn right inta the audience, tryin' ta show those folks that he could really play jazz, wantin' 'em so desperately ta respond ta 'im jus' the way they did when the kid played. But no one was applaudin'. On the contrary they was booin' an' laughin' at 'im, an' some o' 'em was walkin' out. Yet even wit' all that goin' on, Stormy continued playin', livin' in his own world. After all, he'd waited a long time for the chance ta get on stage at Squire's Place an' play jazz, an' now he was finally doin' it.

Then, right inta his second solo chorus, the fireworks start. Wit'out warnin' the kid, wit' his silver sax in hand, leaps from the shadows onta the stage. It all happened so fast Stormy didn't know what hit 'im. While Stormy's buildin' his solo, the kid begins steppin' on his feet, gradually nudgin' 'im off ta the sidelines, an' while he's doin' it, he's all the time blowin' hard an' loud over Stormy's now ragged ad libs which come apart at the seams, jus' as the kid replaces 'em wit' his own more confident an' slick version o' the tune.

An' if that ain't humiliation enough for Stormy, wit' the rhythm section vampin' behind 'im—includin' me on bass, and I couldn't get away now even if I tried—the kid suddenly grabs the microphone, an' in a voice loud enough for everyone ta hear, says ta Stormy, "Now that's how it's supposed ta be done, kid, ya dig? Guess you ain't never been to a real cuttin' contest before. Well, ya done been cut! Ha, ha, haa! Well, no matter. Look kid, ya better go on out there an' git ya some **S-O-U-L** if ya wanna blow jazz on that thang ya call a sax. C'mon back in 'bout ten or fifteen years when ya really have somethang important ta say. By then, if you're lucky, maybe somebody'll truly wanna listen ta ya!!"

There was nothin' me or anybody else coulda done then; it was too late for all that. Knowin' Stormy as I did, I could only imagine how he musta felt bein' put down like that. From up on the stage where I was still jammin', I thought I caughta glimpse 'o my friend, shoulders hunched, grippin' his sax case and headin' hell-bent for the door through the crowd that was still dissin' 'im.

By the time I'd packed up my bass an' left the club, it was dark an' Stormy was nowhere ta be found. I walked all 'round the neighborhood for a while lookin' for 'im, hopin' we'd connect. Somehow that wasn't gonna be, at least not that night. It was already gittin' late an' I needed ta beat feet home. O' all nights, I certainly didn't wanna explain where I'd been, an''specially what I'd been up ta. I didn't need the grief since my folks was never keen on the idea o' my goin' ta Harlem ta play jazz music in the first place. As far as I was now concerned, that was all past history. There was nothin' my parents, or anyone else, could ever say that could stand 'tween me an' my dreams. After this day, I was hooked on playin' jazz; it was as important ta me as breathin' fresh air, an' ya know somethang, it *was* my fresh air.

But Stormy an' what he went through…what did that all mean? Ya had ta wonder, but I've come ta believe that there are no accidents. The longer you're on this planet you'll see!! What happened ta Stormy coulda had some higher purpose. Why else would the Lord have put his hand on 'im an' then have that upstart sax player carry out some o' the work? I'll never know; it's too deep for me, but ya go figure!!

An' speakin' o' that upstart alto sax player, if you're wonderin' whatever became o' 'im, funny, I never did run inta 'im again. After bein' in this business for a while, I've got me a theory 'bout guys like 'im…sure, I know they're out there, but ya usually don't git ta see 'em ev'ry day. Guys like that kid are a flash in the pan, a needle in a haystack. Once in a great while, they'll come 'round an' dazzle ya wit' all their brilliance. Then they're gone, jus' like butterflies, an' ya know you'll never see 'em again. But ya never stop lookin' for 'em. I'll certainly never forget listenin' ta the kid, an' 'specially havin' the opportunity ta jam with 'im. Ya don't ever forget stuff like that!

Despite what had happened, I was flyin' high, after all, I'd made the grade. The band really dug my stuff an' I was even invited back ta sub for Truck, who was goin' out on the road wit' another band. I knew Stormy could find his way home on his own, though, an' after I got on the subway, I really didn't give 'im much thought.

Saxopolis

SURPRISE ENCOUNTERS

Surprise Encounters

The Mentor's Challenge:
To turn a few smoldering embers into a blazing fire
of inspiration and possibility.

~ Harrison Goldberg, in conversation

Living Spirit is the thing I look for most
in music. I want to be thrilled with the wonder of it.

~ Gil Evans

In the meantime, Stormy, believin' his dreams crushed, an' already willin' ta hawk his sax at the first chance he had, wandered for some time through the darkened Harlem streets, goin' from one neighborhood ta the next, hopin' ta forget the events that had caused 'im great shame an' sadness. This tall, skinny kid luggin' his sax case musta made quite a picture 'cause it was rare, 'specially after hours, ta see a white cat roamin' the streets o' Harlem all alone. Nobody messed with 'im, however, an' after a while he said it did 'im real good bein' right where he was, walkin' his mind off things. It was exactly the kind o' warm summer night up here in Harlem that y'all can appreciate. Stormy described it ta a 'T'...people strollin' arm in arm or jus' sittin' out on their stoops, laughin' an' talkin', an' some even huggin' an' kissin'.

Wit'out a definite destination in mind, soon Stormy comes ta this wide avenue y'all know so well. The whole place was buzzin'. He heard the magical sounds o' jazz music again, taxi cabs honkin' their horns everywhere, people hollerin', an' he smelled the pungent aroma o' barbecue. Yeah, Stormy was takin' it all in an' checkin' it all out. The streets was awash in neon-flickerin' signs advertisin':

COFFEE'NDOUGHNUTSCHEAPEATSBEAUTYSALONS NEWSTANDSTATTOOPARLORSMOVIEHOUSESPAWNSHOPSPIZZA BURGERS'NFRIES.

...everythang runnin' together in a blur. But it was the jazz clubs along the strip, their sounds gettin' louder an' more insistent by the minute, that really caught his attention...the saxes: altos, tenors, sopranos an' baritones; bones an' trumpets; pianos; drums; vibes; guitars; their sounds all came bubblin' up 'round 'im. An' that's 'bout the time he started gittin' dizzy...ya see, last time Stormy had anythang in his stomach musta been when we scarfed those dogs while waitin' ta get inta Squire's Place, an' that was ages ago. I can tell ya that he was gittin' tired too; ya don't go luggin' a sax case all over town wit'out puttin' fuel in your engine. So he stops ta rest, an' where was it but right in front o' a well-lit jazz club inta which crowds o' folks was pourin'. I think y'all oughta be pretty familiar wit' this place too, but I won't spoil all your fun; you'll figure it out soon.

While Stormy's leanin' 'gainst his sax case, up from the sidewalk comes the sound I dig so much: sizzlin' cymbals keepin' company wit' a walkin' bass...but that doesn't quite catch his ear until the sound o' a tenor saxophone, unlike anythang he'd ever heard before starts wailin', an' I mean *WAILIN'*, above a stridin' piana. That was what brought Stormy back ta life, ya can believe it!! An' then there was that message on the neon sign, ya know, the one out in front o' the club that read: **The Bass Clef—Featuring Jazz Greats from Here, There, and Out of Nowhere.**

...an' while he's lookin' at it he remembers what his folks had said earlier that same day ta discourage 'im from goin' ta Harlem: "Harlem is nowhere for a boy like ya ta be!" But this time, Stormy doesn't mutter his thoughts ta 'imself. He takes 'em ta the street, an' in a voice loud enough for anyone passin' by The Bass Clef ta hear, he defiantly announces, *"Well, at least it's my **SOMEPLACE**, Nowhere, an' surely I will be **SOMEBODY** there!!"*

Wit' that declaration, he merges inta the crowd, an' still grippin' his sax case, he's carried along downstairs ta another world. It's there that Stormy forgets his disgrace an' his rumblin' belly. Instead, he becomes caught up in the most extraordinary tenor sax playin' he ever coulda imagined was possible comin' from someone on this planet.

He told me that there was somethang otherworldly 'bout it, even the light was diff'rent. There was a strange golden glow comin' from the direction o' the stage that backlit all the players, but 'specially the sax man. "His glow was definitely the brightest," Stormy said, "an' if you looked closely, it was even givin' off sparks, I swear!"

His name was Dr. Saxx, that's all anyone knew 'bout him. He was an ol' wiry black man wit' spectacles an' a neatly trimmed salt an' pepper beard. "He coulda been a professor or somethang...hard ta figure this vibe I was pickin' up," Stormy said. "From the buzz in the room, ya could tell that before that night, no one in The Bass Clef had ever seen or heard o' this cat...but MAN, could he play!!...An' what a show he put on frontin' his group o' piana, bass, an' drums. The way Stormy described it, I sure wish I'd been there. It was as if time hung suspended an' the four walls o' the club disappeared...all that existed was pure music that rose up singin' out o' the cat's sax like some dimly understood story, almost as old as time hitself. Accordin' ta Stormy, the language o' that story had real power an' it reached the sacred place Stormy'd shut down after the incident at Squire's Place.

While he's diggin' on the music, Stormy thinks he sees a shinin' gold music note...that's right, you heard me the first time...I said a real *LIVE* note!...but this one's got a smilin' face an' even a body wit' danglin' arms 'n legs...an' lo an' behold, it's comin',...comin' right out o' the bell o' Dr. Saxx's horn. Can you believe it...WOOOWEEE!!! Stormy's gotta be trippin'...I mean, this ain't the sort o' thang that your average music note does every day; they usually prefer bein' heard an' not seen if ya know what I'm sayin'.

From the git-go this musical note had its own agenda...an' there wasn't anythang gonna keep it from accomplishin' that work. For a while, the note jus' hovered above the bell o' Dr. Sax's horn, checkin' thangs out, then suddenly it sees Stormy hangin' out in the back o' the room an' starts dancin' through the darkness towards 'im...now, that couldna been an easy thang ta do 'cause the note had ta git 'round a whole lot o' folks before it could reach Stormy. But like I said, this note wasn't like any other note, an' it definitely had a mind o' its own.

Now I've given this a lot o' thought over the years, an' you can call me crazy if you'd like, but the real truth accordin' ta Forest Tune is: Stormy

Already Knew This Note!! That's right, ya heard me!..Stormy knew this note better than the back o' his hand...now I don't mean he'd actually been face-ta-face wit' it...what I'm talkin' 'bout here is Stormy was the one who created it, not Dr. Saxx...sure the sax man give it form, but 'twas Stormy's spirit ta play jazz that gave it life!!

So while Stormy's listenin' real good an' hard ta the music, he happens ta look up an' see the same note—the one that he'd seen moments earlier near the bell o' Dr. Saxx's horn—now comin' at 'im all bright an' shiny wit' its smile lightin' up the way. He can't believe what he's seein'. Now he knows he's losin' his mind for real an' he looks nervously all 'round him ta see if anyone else has noticed. But everythang appears ta be in its place, jus' folks out havin' fun listenin' ta great jazz music...so Stormy goes back ta listenin', really concentratin' on the music...pretendin' that he doesn't see this note that's still movin', though not nearly as fast as before, in his direction. What Stormy doesn't know is that he couldna stopped that note from travelin' ta 'im any more than he couldna stopped the music comin' out o' Dr. Saxx's horn if he'd truly wanted ta. The livin' note was jazz music come alive!!...an' it was already an inseparable part o' Stormy.

The music!! Yeahh, that's the place where Stormy needed ta be. The ballad Dr. Saxx was playin' was real D-E-L-I-C-I-O-U-S...warm an' fuzzy notes all quiverin' over lush piana chords, massaged by the deep an' hypnotic throb o' a string bass lightly dusted by brushes...Stormy loses 'imself in it. Then comes the crescendo, wit' the band all risin' up as one voice headin' ta the climax. By now Stormy's skin's a-tinglin'.

Wit' the sax master drawin' every last ounce o' beauty an' blues out o' the melody, Stormy looks up an' sees the livin' note not more than ten feet from 'im...fact is, he even looks it right in the eye an' there, jus' at the exact moment he feels the note reach out an' touch his heart, Stormy sees 'imself...big as life...an' plain as day...an' then, that note was gone...out o' there...jus' like that...in the blink o' an eye!!!

An' so was the gig. Folks began leavin' soon as the lights came on, but not Stormy. He was still reelin' from what he'd been hearin', an' 'specially from what he'd jus' been seein'. He sat there for a bit lettin' it all soak in, but eventually he did get up ta go, an' as he made his way ta the club's

door, he ran smack inta Dr. Saxx—I mean he didn't knock 'im over—they jus'
connected. You can call it fate, kismet, or any o' those other names that all
mean the same thang. By this time the club is empty o' all the other folks.

"Please allow me to introduce myself," the elder musician began
in soft measured tones. "I'm Dr. Saxx, and you must be Stormy Keys. Now
don't look so startled, Stormy. Your mind isn't playing tricks!

"But how on earth did you know my name?" asked Stormy. "Let's
just say that it was Jazz, the mermaid from The Sea of Time in The Land
called Song, who told me to be on the lookout for ya," said Dr. Saxx. "It was
after you bought the horn at the pawn shop; she gave me your name and a
pretty good description of you. I knew that sooner or later you'd be paying
me a visit. Of course, all this is written off the staff; this is not your average
musical experience. You might just say that I've been watching for ya, and
as you can see, I had no trouble picking you out of the crowd."

At the mention of the mermaid, Stormy just happened to look
down the length of Dr. Saxx's horn until his eyes came to rest on the bell.
To his amazement, there was the same engraved scene with the mermaid,
tropical island, sailing ship and all, that graced the bell of his own recently
purchased tenor sax. In fact, Stormy decided that both horns were
identical—even the colors were the same.

But before he could dwell on it too much, Dr. Saxx continued in
his deep bell-like voice, so rich that it mirrored the resonant musical voice
which moments earlier had sprung from his tenor.

"You didn't know it, Stormy, but that very first day you opened your
sax case, I was right there in the room with you. I saw the love of music in
your eyes. Later on, as that day grew into years, I felt a growing respect in
your heart and sensed your unspoken commitment and desire to become a
jazz tenor saxophonist, the very best you could possibly be. And on that day,
you forged an inseparable bond with me. To you, I am the past, present, and
future of all music that issues from the saxophone. That day, the day when
you chose to learn the music of jazz, I was born within you. I am the African
American voice of the saxophone, the soul of this instrument!"

"Though I've lived in past musical worlds, I now move with you,
sometimes forward, sometimes backward, through space and time,

but never once forgetting to remember and honor my revered ancestors. After all, it was their sacrifice which brought me to this special musical place. Remember that jazz music celebrates the freedom and spontaneous creative expression of a race of people who refused to die in an alien land. In spite of their enslavement, they created a heroic new language, a musical speech influenced by the songs heard in the slave master's church. Spirituals and gospel evolved and were joined at the hip with the blues, a heart-wrenching lament born from the harsh daily servitude visited upon them as they toiled in fields under a blazing and relentless sun. All this new music tied them to the African soil of their fathers and their forefathers, and make no mistake, that sound you heard comin' from my horn was forged on the anvil of my people's travail!"

"Even while I was playing, I was studying you and I could plainly tell by the way you were listening to me that you wanted real bad to play this black man's music, though I sensed something might have happened along the way to discourage you from continuing. After all, I had to see if your desire was still strong enough. And that's when I chose to entrust to your care a magical musical note. 'Course, and you probably didn't know this at the time, I made you work extra hard for that note, you know. I made you reach down deep into the empty space with your whole inner being and will that note to you. You did real well, too; shows you wanted it badly enough, but I still had to be sure."

"Now Stormy, you treat that note with respect, and eventually it will lead you to other notes even more beautiful. These notes, all of them, come from a long way off and from a long time ago when drums were kings—long before these horns started talking to you. If you handle them with care and reverence, in time they're going to come singing from your horn, and then folks are really going to start falling in love with your sound, believe me!"

Stormy's eyes were getting bigger by the moment when he receives the elder musician's challenge. "Stormy, everyone has their story, so what's yours? You must go find and live it from beginning to end. Sing straight from the heart and play your horn. Live to spread joy and all that's true by building bridges and healing pain. Now I ask, what could be a more positive refrain? That's when you'll find, and I'm telling you, the sound you're looking for is none other than **You!!** That's your story and your song, that's who **You** are and where **You** belong!"

"Now it's going to be up to you to get your chops happening. Continue to perfect your craft through hard work and careful study. It's going to take a lifetime of dedication, but if you diligently practice your long tones, eventually you'll form a bridge connecting your musical spirit to the universe of all men and women. Wherever they may be, your spirit will bring them together, uniting them in peace and universal harmony. It's about time you started preparing for that ultimate gig **NOW!** If you really want to be a jazz saxophonist, you can't just sit at home forever practicing and waiting for the phone to ring. No, you have to get yourself out there. It's time for you to show off your stuff, but you better be plenty hungry for it."

"Dig this, jam's the only real food that's truly going to hold you until you get there. I mean, I'm advising you to go out now and find some serious cats like yourself to jam with and just play it straight from the heart, the best you can, and don't worry about anything. If you really love it, it'll come out of your horn that way. Soon enough, folks are going to start digging on your sound. You'll see. First of all though, you have to get a tone happening with only a few notes. That's the key to your real voice, and you want it to be instantly recognized. Above all, be a singing player-let your voice sing out through your axe like all those important tenor men, Cats like Coleman Hawkins, Ben Webster, Lester Young, Chu Berry, Ike Quebec, Dexter Gordon, Sonny Rollins, John Coltrane, Paul Gonsalves, and Illinois Jacquet, to name but a few. Once you get them down, along with knowing and feeling the blues, eventually you'll be on your own like me, telling your story too, putting your signature, Stormy Keys, to it while some bad rhythm section backs you up. And remember, never stop listening to the cats you're playing with, after all, it's their story too, and you'll be drawing inspiration, building from them every step of the way. In that way you'll be free to move in any direction you want. That's what playing jazz is all about—not only using your own imagination but communicating and interacting with other cats is important too!"

"Never stop trying to keep your music fresh and alive. That comes from taking chances. Be a risk taker. It'll pay off. Now, about this thing called *SOUL* that somebody at a jam session said you don't have, let me just set you straight on that one. Listen carefully. We, all of us, already have the *K-E-Y-S* to the kingdom!! Only thing we have to do is find the right door and trust that our key fits. It just takes each of us a certain amount of time and hard work. In the end, when your chops are together, the best music will come through you by itself; you'll hardly realize that it's happening to you. And that's because if you've done it right, you'll become the intended vessel for a higher power working through you. But you have to let it happen, and most importantly, you have to really want it."

"One last word about what we sax players refer to as our set up, you know, the combination of mouthpiece, reed and ligature. It's always been a personal thing, but you'll hear a lot of cats promoting this or that mouthpiece and younger unseasoned players will always be susceptible 'cause it's normal and cool to want to sound like one of the Greats. While a certain amount of experimenting with your gear can be a good thing, in the long run it can also make you crazy...and just because you have the same set up as one of your heroes doesn't mean that you're going to sound like him. No siree! My advice to you, and I'm speaking from experience, find a mouthpiece-metal or hard rubber-that works for you and stick with it. If every time you hear a great jazz saxophonist and keep switching mouthpieces-reeds and ligatures too- you'll never apprehend an original sound, discover your authentic voice. Study these cats, celebrate 'em, even borrow some of their licks, but develop your own personal expression, your voice and not someone else's...end of story!"

"Play then, this language of my people's survival. Celebrate it and let your horn voice sing out loud and true. Wherever there may be men enslaved, eventually your music will reach their ears and restore their hope for a long-awaited freedom! Suddenly Dr. Saxx looks at a wall clock and announces: "I almost forgot. I'm going to have to run if I'm going to make my next gig on time. It's a recording date and you don't want to keep those cats waitin'. But just one more thing that you'll surely be needin' for the road, believe me. You might call it a little assist from *The Living Spirit*, if you know what I mean!"

Stormy catches the sax man's wink before the elder urges:

"So get out there and have some fun with the music! I'll be keeping my eyes on you, and you'd better believe I'll be listening to you; I don't miss a trick!"

At that moment the room suddenly fills with a blinding flash of golden light, then instantly everything goes dark. By the time the lights go back on, Stormy is sitting alone at the table. The sax man has vanished. On the table in front of his vacant seat, a shining *Golden Reed* powerfully glows. Silently and resolutely picking up the glittering keepsake, he grabs his saxophone case and emerges into a city coming reluctantly alive from its uneasy nocturnal slumber. Stormy couldn't have been more thrilled. If he'd always wanted to be a jazz saxophonist, those words spoken by Dr. Saxx that night forever sealed his destiny and from the music he'd heard earlier, he sensed something fantastic was about to unfold.

On the day following his amazing adventure, Stormy comes ta my house lookin' for me. As usual, I was off someplace, but later my mother told me he had come 'round, an' she said, "Never, never" had she seen 'im so worked up. Well, naturally, that got me curious. I finally caught up with 'im a couple o' days later, an' he gave me the low down. It's sort o' strange that after we connected an' he shared all this far out stuff wit' me, Stormy an' his family just plain up an' dropped out o' sight. Not so much as a word from the cat. It's as if he vanished from the face o' the earth, wit' not even a trace. I'd even heard tell he'd moved out o' state, maybe ta California, an' as far as I was concerned, that was a pretty good disappearin' act.

As time passed, I'd wonder what ever happened ta my friend an' if there was any truth ta that golden reed thang. An' I wasn't the only one thinkin' 'bout it either. Seemed like just 'bout everyone I told Stormy's story ta wanted ta know if the cat really had Dr. Saxx's golden reed. An' if so, did that mean he now had some kind o' magical power like no other sax player on earth had ever had before? Would it, for example, be possible for him ta take 25 consecutive solo choruses—each one more original an' powerful than the one that came before? An' would he now be able ta hear thangs so far beyond the imagination o' anyone wit' God-given ears?

Along with these crazy notions, I started thinkin' 'bout whether that magical power could run out when you least expected it. Isn't magic like that! One minute it's here, an' suddenly in the next instant it's gone, jus' like that. So you'd better treat that gift wit' respect 'cause you never know when you'd be losin' it. I had no doubt whatsoever wherever Stormy was, that if he had that reed, he'd surely be takin' full advantage o' it!

Then o' course, there was Dr. Saxx 'imself. Yeah, I have ta admit that ever since I heard Stormy's tale, I've been on the lookout for the "good Doctor." But I can tell ya for a fact that I've never run inta 'im, not even a trace of 'im either. Like Stormy, he jus' vanished inta thin air. I even spread the word 'mong the brothers I hang wit' in the Apple an' believe me, 'tween us we pretty much have the whole jazz scene covered—gigs, after hour sessions, studios, even certain cafes an' waterin' holes in the off hours—all kinds o' places where a heavy jazz sax cat like that would likely show up. No Dice— nobody'd ever even heard of 'im. Still, an' ya can call it my gut feelin' if ya want, I have real reason ta believe that Stormy didn't jus' make this cat up. In fact, it was a year later that I knew at last that I was hot on Dr. Saxx's trail.

I was on the subway an' this guy sittin' next ta me gits up an' leaves his newspaper on the seat. Since I still had a ways ta go before my stop, I reached over an' picked up what turned out ta be the Leisure and Arts section o' the Wall Street Journal. Imagine my surprise when turnin' the first page I come face ta face wit' a headline that reads: **"Young Men with Horns Learn by Listening to Elders."** An' if that wasn't enough, smack in the middle o' the story's third column was a drawin' o' a saxophone wit' the words, **"Jazz Mentors"** opposite it. Even if I'd never actually seen his name mentioned in the article, that headline alone mighta been all I needed ta convince me that there really was someone out there known as Dr. Saxx, a mentor exactly like the one Stormy had described ta me.

But wait a minute; that's not all! A couple o' months after findin' that story, I happened ta be checkin' out the music section in my neighborhood newsstand. I picked up a copy o' the #1 international jazz magazine, "Down Beat," an' on the cover, larger than life, is a picture o' this well-known African American tenor sax player. It fit Stormy's description o' Dr. Saxx ta a 'T', salt an' pepper beard, spectacles an' all. The article raved 'bout the cat's sound, said it "launched a thousand horns," and in fact it went on ta say that "there was this growin' consensus in the jazz community that this man was the model for young saxophonists ta look up ta."

Now I know you're gonna tell me his name ain't Dr. Saxx. It don't matter! Look, I don't care how many aliases the cat's got, or even if he's usin' disguises when he shows up at his gigs. The fact is, the cat's always been here, right under our noses, in the trenches, carryin' on the work he's supposed ta be doin' on the planet—playin' his horn an' handin' down a valuable tradition. An' it's time y'all be hearin' 'bout him and tunin' in, **ya dig?** So without further adieu, we're gonna give y'all a jazz tune that'll make "the Good Dr." proud. Easy listenin'...One, two, ...one, two, three, four..."

Now it happens that this same summer's night, one might say coincidentally, as Stormy, his ubiquitous sax case in hand, passes by The Bass Clef, he notices a familiar name on the club's marquee. It had been many years since he last saw or even heard from his former teenage pal. Now here he was, Forest Tune, actually appearing at the famous Bass Clef, the very place where Stormy himself had had the most unforgettable experience of his life. So naturally he is more than a little curious to hook up with his friend again, and especially there. However, what is significant is that on this particular night, Forest's sax player has elected to join another band which was departing immediately for a more lucrative overseas gig.

There is hardly time for Forest to find a suitable replacement. Though his rhythm section is more than capable of holding their own in any given performance situation, Forest is daunted by the prospect of opening before a sold-out audience without the compelling lead voice of a tenor saxophone to inspire his trio. Still, the show must go on and Forest, a true professional, knows that he has to rise to the occasion.

By the time Stormy Keys, now a bearded young man, reenters The Bass Clef, he himself is also a full-fledged and working jazz musician, though not nearly as financially successful as Forest. In the parlance of jazz musicians, one might say that Stormy has "paid his dues." During the past ten plus years, Dr. Saxx's legacy of instruction and the gift of the mysterious *Golden Reed* have greatly influenced and given purpose to his life. From the appearance and expression on his face, it is evident that Stormy has lived the music and not just practiced it on his horn. He has taken his mentor's lessons to heart. These included "jamming" with as many players as he possibly could, particularly those who inspired and challenged him.

Of course, he also continued to listen to and absorb the recorded legacy and achievements left behind by the great jazz masters.

Making his way assuredly through the smoky din, Stormy is met by the welcoming sight of his friend Forest on a floodlit stage, a string bass cradled snugly in his big arms. Rocking back and forth upon his heels, the bass man, as if in a trance, growls with enthusiasm while he plays, never once looking up, yet competently directing his trio through some hidden channel of energy that seems to bind them all together.

Stormy can hardly contain his excitement. Without the slightest hesitation, and with a great confidence born of his seasoned musical experiences, he quickly unpacks and assembles his horn. First, the neck strap. Next, he attaches a hard rubber mouthpiece to the curved neck of the instrument. Finally, reaching into a shirt pocket next to his heart, he extricates a thin glittering object, a sliver the exact size and dimensions of a bamboo tenor saxophone reed. After carefully moistening it with his saliva, he meticulously places this *Golden Reed* upon the mouthpiece and then fastens a metal ligature securely to it.

Instantly the horn radiates a golden energy which seems to clear a brightening path for Stormy through the dimly lit room and directly to the stage. The glow, however, is visible only to his eyes, since it is he alone who has activated the energy from the *Golden Reed*, Dr. Saxx's inspired gift. As he reaches the stage, and although there has yet to be an invitation or any formal announcement for him to do so by the band's leader, Stormy resolutely ascends and takes his place confidently among the musicians who nonchalantly continue their playing. With his back to Forest, who is anchored solidly between the piano and drums, Stormy temporarily remains anonymous to his friend. But no sooner has the piano player finished his solo than he steps forward and launches soulfully into his own solo on the famous Green/Heyman tune, "Out of Nowhere," with which he has demonstrated earlier in his life that he is more than just casually familiar.

The room suddenly comes alive. Whistling and shouting words of encouragement, the audience favorably and enthusiastically responds to this stranger's dramatic entrance. The band, however, seems to take Stormy's sudden interruption in stride, hardly registering any unusual change in its casual demeanor, despite the fact that the horn man exuberantly wails among them. But even so, moment to moment, their assured accompaniment begins to gather a new and dynamic level of energy which has already begun to feed the audience.

It was becoming obvious to Forest and his fellow musicians that in this young white guy's playing could be detected the distinct and compelling voices of the most influential African American tenor saxophonists, titans like Coleman Hawkins, Ben Webster, Lester Young, Dexter Gordon, Sonny Rollins, and John Coltrane. Most importantly, they heard this young tenor man stepping out confidently from behind the shadows of those giants to assert his own personality, telling a story which bore his own unique, yet blues-based stamp. The story, effortlessly told with soft, warm and furry tones, purrs easily from the stranger's horn. Forest and his band take note that while the sax man appears to have an unlimited supply of free and spontaneous ideas, at no time does he allow his improvisation to get too cluttered, or to repeat phrases and ideas that had come before.

On the contrary, not only does this performer seem to have an unlimited repository of fresh ideas at his disposal, he also takes the time to honor the silences around him. When he stops, sometimes for an instant or two, and at other times for longer, the plush phrases of the rhythm section of bass, drums, and piano bubble up to the surface; the sax man seems to derive energy from the other players. When he resumes his playing, it seems to reflect and even expand upon ideas he is absorbing from his bandmates' musical vocabulary. Playfully, with a sense of humor as well as pathos, he weaves his ideas into imaginative patterns and phrases evoking moods, colors, and even dreamscapes.

From time to time he ingeniously inserts fragments of quotations from the masters into the fabric of his solo while at no time during his playing does he ever get lost in the tune's changes, or lose sight of the melody which serves as a beacon to light his way home. Here is a musician who seems to be truly enjoying himself. To that extent, he appears to be a lightning rod for the energy that seems to come on its own behalf, singing and rejoicing, from his horn. The sax man might be intoning from the very wellspring of an ancient human memory.

Halfway through Stormy's third, and what was to be his final explosive chorus with the tune, "Out of Nowhere," with the rhythm section playing their up tempo swing version at full throttle and cooking feverishly below the tenor man's crisp, round, and full-sounding notes, Stormy looks up to see a great smile of recognition suddenly illuminate Forest's face. By the time Stormy takes the melody joyfully home, the audience is up and out of their seats wildly applauding. Something from Forest's eyes, and the look of brotherhood and shared respect which they seem to convey, is enough to convince Stormy that at last he has found his *Living Spirit*, and is returning triumphantly home with it.

Almost immediately, Forest grabs the microphone but has to wait a bit before the excited audience settles down so he can address them. In the half darkness, with the applause beating wildly in his ears, Stormy closes his eyes and lets his thoughts drift back more than ten years earlier. It had certainly been quite a journey and he had come full circle from the humiliating experience he had endured during that first jam session in Harlem. But this was really only just a beginning and would probably last him a lifetime, or two or three for that matter, if he were ever able to return again once he departed this earth. Out of the corner of his thoughts, Stormy hears Forest speak, and so, quickly, he returns to the earthly present world of The Bass Clef to take in his friend's hope-filled words.

First, Forest speaks directly to his old friend, "Hey, my brother, I gotta admit, ya had me fooled! Not only did your playin' completely blow me away, but I couldna even tell it was ya behind all that facial hair. 'Tween the hot glare o' the floods an' all this smoke an' stuff, it'd be tough ta know your own Momma if she was ta walk in here. In the end though, there was somethang 'bout ya that gave ya away. Then to the audience, he says, "On behalf o' The Bass Clef, I'm Forest Tune, an' ya'll been listenin' ta Brothers o' the Treble featurin'—for the very first time from Nowhere, ha ha, haaa, excuse me, I mean from **SOMEPLACE,** Nowhere—the one an' only...Stormy Keys...on tenor saxophone. Yeahh, put your hands together for 'im...**Man, oh Man, this here's one SOULFUL CAT!!** Somethin' tells me you're gonna be hearin' a lot more from this brother in the future, so jus' stay tuned. Ya hear?!"

Pianological (for Bill Evans)

NO END TO THE POSSIBILITIES

⊕ No End to the Possibilities

*"I believe that the day will come when
all God's children from bass black to treble white will be
significant on the Constitution's keyboard."*

~ Martin Luther King, Jr.
San Francisco, California, 1956

The *Golden Reed!* **Hey,** it's been years so don't tell me you're still harpin' on that one again. No, honestly, I can tell ya I've never seen it, but there's really no reason ta, at least not now. Look, I heard Stormy blow an' that's proof enough! An' so did a lot o' others. Folks who was in the Clef that night are still talkin' 'bout how that white guy could play, an' that was deep in the heart o' Harlem too. What I *can* tell ya is that there was no gimmicks—jus' the love the cat's always had in his heart for the music an' his wantin' ta share it. It's as simple as that! An' that's the way it came out o' his horn, like liquid gold.

Well, you can call it fate, but right after our historic reunion at The Bass Clef, Stormy an' me hooked us up a real class act, three horns up front o' a killer rhythm section. On top o' that, we added us a guitar 'cause that's the big thang right now. Our new sounds are jus' killin' 'em, don't matter where we go: Europe, Africa, Japan, Australia or right here in the States; there's all our albums ta prove it, an' they're sellin' like hot cakes. I understand the stores can hardly keep 'em in stock, they're that popular. An' after Stormy came on board, we went from being called "Brothers o' the Treble" to "The Brotherhood o' Man" 'cause we thought it came a little closer ta capturin' the spirit o' what jazz music's really about—bringin' all people together swingin' under one sun.

Still, by far the biggest kick we git is when we're invited ta teach jazz in schools, colleges an' universities 'round the country. Sort o' makes us feel like we be changin' places wit' Dr. Saxx, an' that's a real important part, bein' in a place where you can pass on this wonderful gift, makin' a diff'rence. Naturally we tell our students the authentic history o' the music an' its African American connection, well, at least up ta the present, an' even that's constantly changin'. Then there's some real important technical stuff they're surely gonna need ta help 'em git their chops an' keep 'em, mostly scales an' things like that. Ours is a different approach though. Learnin' ta play jazz isn't always 'bout fancy licks an' tricks. That's jus' a very small part o' it. We try ta leave these students hungry an' curious enough ta find out what's really motivatin' 'em inside ta want ta play this music. Once they've figured all that out, 'long wit' assimilatin' the voices o' the greats, then hopefully they're well on the way ta discoverin' their own unique voices, the signature o' their inner bein'. Soon enough, they'll be joyously puttin' it out there for people ta hear...**so stay tuned, ya dig!**

*But I've
got to keep
experimenting.*

*I feel that I'm just
beginning.*

*I have part of
what I'm looking
for in my grasp
but not all.*

~ John Coltrane

Refrain in Black and White

Jazz After Hours

AFTER HOURS

Imagine If Jazz Were Like Baseball
Homage to the Greats

Imagine If Jazz Were Like Baseball
Oh...oh what a game!
We'd be rooting for hip players
but not of Babe Ruth's fame.

If jazz were a game like baseball
just imagine the line-up there could be:
Satchmo; The Brute and The Beautiful, Hawk, Trane and Bird; The Sound;
PeeWee, Monk and Diz; Cannonball, the Count, King, Duke, Baron, Kid Ory,
Sassy, Flip, Stix, Bix, and Fats.

Instead of hitting fastballs, our heroes would be swinging
melodious music notes miles high, way into the sky,
creating stars, bright new planets
where their souls could thrive.

Refrain:
        Lester leaps
        Satchmo trumpets
        Ella scats
        Bird flies
        Not hitting dusty baseballs
        But swinging melodious music notes miles high!

Now consider this scenario, especially if you're a jazz aficionado:
Its bases loaded with two outs in the bottom of the ninth,
three to two count on the batter and the game is all tied up.

Then back to the plate he steps,
Cannonball Adderley, his fearsome alto
brushing a wide chest.
The crowd yells, "Mercy, Mercy,"
and you can hear that horn man blowing loud and steady,
swinging mightily with his sax.

Over the stands and right out of the park
Cannon's crisp, clear notes rip the pitch to the max.
"It's a grand slam," the crowd roars,
while in the dugout the rhythm section jams.

In case you don't believe us,
just listen closely.
Late at night and up towards heaven
you'll hear these great jazz folks
wailing in all their glory.
Chorus after chorus, each one outdoing the last,
piano, bass and drums sure have themselves a formidable task.

Back to earth here at Shea Stadium
we can let our minds wander and our dreams drift out.

If jazz were a game like baseball
just imagine the line-up there could be
Satchmo; The Brute and the Beautiful, Hawk, Trane, and Bird; The Sound;
PeeWee, Monk and Diz; Cannonball, The Count, King, Duke, Baron, Kid Ory,
And how about that glorious gal called
Lady Day!

But hold on...we're not though yet;
the opposing team has much to fear when
The Steamer, Slam, Slide, Bunk, Lucky, Zoot, Fathead, Lockjaw,
The Lion, Jug, Long Tall Dex, Illinois, Philly Joe, Cleanhead, Chu,
and a Mohegan-sporting pitcher,
Newk the Saxophone Colossus, appears.

So trust us when we tell you
there isn't an outfielder on this planet
who's going to bring down those notes once these jazz cats send them
flying!

Refrain:
        Lester leaps
        Satchmo trumpets
        Ella scats
        Bird flies
        Not hitting dusty baseballs
        But swinging melodious music notes miles high!

        (Fade out w/music...)

        ...Not hitting dusty baseballs,
        But swinging melodious music notes miles high!
        ...Not hitting dusty baseballs...

        (Pause before continuing to the end)

        ...But Swinging Beautiful Music Notes Miles High!

Musician Nickname Reference

Satchmo
Louis Armstrong
Trumpet
August 4, 1901–July 6, 1971

The Brute and The Beautiful
Benjamin Francis Webster,
aka "Frog"
Tenor saxophone
March 27, 1909–September 20, 1973

Hawk
Coleman Hawkins,
aka "Bean"
Tenor saxophone
November 21, 1904–May 19, 1969

Trane
John Williams Coltrane
Tenor and soprano saxophone
September 23, 1926–July 17, 1967

Bird
Charlie Parker
Alto saxophone
August 29, 1920–March 12, 1955

The Sound
Stan Getz
Tenor saxophone
February 2, 1927–June 6, 1991

PeeWee
Charles Ellsworth Russell
Clarinet and saxophone
March 27, 1906–February 15, 1969

Monk
Thelonious Sphere Monk
Piano and composer
October 10, 1917–February 17, 1982

Diz
John Birks "Dizzy" Gillespie
Trumpet, bandleader and composer
October 21, 1917–January 6, 1993

Cannonball
Julian Edwin Adderley
Alto saxophone
September 15, 1928–August 8, 1975

The Count
William James Basie
Piano, organ, bandleader and
composer
August 21, 1904–April 26, 1984

King
Joseph Nathan Oliver
Cornet, pioneer of the mute in jazz,
and bandleader
December 19, 1881–April 10, 1938

Duke
Duke Ellington
Piano, conductor, and composer
April 29, 1899–May 24, 1974

Baron
Charles Mingus Jr.
Double bass, bandleader and
composer
April 22, 1922–January 5, 1979

Kid Ory
Edward Ory
Trombone, bandleader and composer
December 25, 1886–January 23, 1973

Sassy
Sara Lois Vaughn
American jazz singer and pianist
March 27, 1924–April 3, 1990

Flip Phillips
Joseph Edward Filippelli
Tenor saxophone and clarinet
March 26, 1915–August 17, 2001

Stix
Nesbert Hooper
Drums
August 15, 1938–

Bix
Leon Bismark Beiderbecke
Cornet, piano, and composer
March 10, 1903–August 6, 1931

Fats
Theodore Navarro
Trumpet
September 24, 1923–July 6, 1950

Pres/Prez
Lester Willis Young
Tenor saxophone and clarinet
August 27, 1909–March 15, 1959

Ella
Ella Jane Fitzgerald
Jazz singer
April 25, 1917–June 15, 1996

Miles
Miles Dewey Davis III
Trumpet, bandleader and composer
May 26, 1926–September 28, 1991

Lady Day
Billie Holiday (formerly Eleanora
Fagan)
Jazz singer
April 7, 1915–July17, 1959

The Steamer
Stanley Levey
Drums
April 5, 1926–April 19, 2005

Slam
Leroy Eliot Stewart
Double bass
September 21, 1914–December 10,
1987

Slide
Locksley Wellington Hampton
Trombone, composer and arranger
April 21, 1932–

Bunk
Willie Gary Johnson
Trumpet
December 27, 1879–July 7, 1949

Lucky
Eli Thompson
Tenor and soprano saxophone
June 16, 1924–July 30, 2005

Zoot
John Haley Sims
Tenor and soprano saxophone
October 29, 1925–March 23, 1985

Fathead
David Newman
Tenor saxophone and flute
February 24, 1933–January 20, 2009

Lockjaw
Eddie Davis
Tenor saxophone
March 22, 1922–November 3, 1986

The Lion
William "Willie" Henry Joseph Bonaparte
Bertholoff Smith
Stride piano
November 23, 1893–April 18, 1973

Jug
Eugene Ammons
Tenor saxophone
April 14, 1925–August 6, 1974

Long Tall Dex
Dexter Gordon
Tenor saxophone
February 27, 1923–April 25, 1990

Rabbit
Cornelius "Johnny" Hodges
Alto saxophone
July 25,1907–May 11, 1970

Illinois
Jean-Baptiste Jacquet
Tenor saxophone
October 31, 1922–July 22, 2004

Philly Joe
Joseph Rudolph Jones
Drums
July 15, 1923–August 30, 1985

Cleanhead
Eddie Vinson
Alto saxophone and blues shouter
December 18, 1917–July 2, 1988

Chu
Leon Brown Berry
Tenor saxophone
September 13, 1908–October 30, 1941

Newk
Theodore Walter Rollins
(said to resemble Don "Newk" Newcombe,
former American League pitcher with the
Brooklyn Dodgers)
Tenor saxophone
September 7, 1930–

Jazz

jazz faces
That Launched
AFRICA
READING, WRITING, AND RHYTHM-A-NING
Music's as good as food for c
JOE HENDERSON
"And that's why the people are ready for this music. Everybody wants it, they're ready for change, and they're ready for positive change, and they're ready to start trying to get together. They're tired of fighting each other, they're tired of being white and black. People are ready to be Americans, and that's why it's time for jazz."
"I think playing the saxophone is what I'm supposed to be doing on this planet. It's the best way I know that I can make the largest number of people happy, and get for myself the largest amount of happiness."
"I was supposed to be a doctor, my family had planned that. But I heard Prez when I was 13, and then Dex when I was 14. That's when I starte Before I turned 15, Bird was the one that infected me with
JAZZ
J•A•Z•Z
EDUCATION
Resurrecting a Wondrous Craft
OBITUARIES
Tenor sax player Dexter Gordon dies
OF NOWHERE
By PETER WATROUS
150 Years Of The Saxophone
"I mean, I'm a saxophone player,
Where do I go from here? Wh do to continue to improve? Ho that next level of communications multitude of improvisation met
WORDS CAN BE DEFINED BY OTHER WORDS. MUSIC CANNOT BE DEFINED BY OTHER SOUNDS BECAUSE NO TWO SOUNDS EXACTLY ALIKE.
"I think the real challenge is carrying your horn around 80 years, playing all your life with no excesses, no drug habit, no notoriety, just quietly going about your business as a super musician"
BLUE
As a teen-ager, Freeman and his friends used to sneak into clubs to hear the likes of trumpeter Louis Armstrong and pianist Earl "Fatha" Hines.
DEXTER GORDON Roost, New York, 1948
Foote believes that jazz is, most importantly, communication. He told John Graham in a 1970 interview, "There's something about the very basic best of jazz, something about the blues, that communicates from one person to another."
Sonny Rollins
To the tune o' He played that sad raggy tune like Sweet Blues! Coming from a black man's soul. O Blues!

Jazz music, a uniquely American-born cultural art form, offers a successful living example, a social model which uses improvisational language coupled with human vitality to create, between its players and listeners alike, an inspired dialogue and spirit of cooperation, engendering compassion and understanding.

Throughout the world, wherever men and women yearn to be free to express themselves creatively and in concert with other like-minded individuals, Jazz music stands as a living symbol of freedom, providing the very noblest form of human communication that, at its best, defines a true democratic society.

~ Harrison Goldberg

Jazz Faces That Launched a Thousand Horns

Masque de Venice

Reflections on the Music of Inclusion

Elijah Carreiro, a guitarist and frequent collaborator with this saxophonist/ author, reflects on the unique improvisational music that the two have created. Whatever one chooses to label their music, the democratic philosophy of inclusion germane to jazz informs their communication.

"I think our playing together is natural and organic...it's very expressive and we tend to carry on a musical conversation with our instruments.
It's exciting and new every time...we have a knack for exploring new ideas on the spot.
We both love to improvise, which keeps us on our toes and delivers an element of the unexpected to our audience.

We always find ways to build and release tension throughout our sets...
It's diverse, yet we have developed a unique sound together...
We push each other creatively while maintaining a balance of musical boundaries and respect...
I think we're both comfortable with our instruments to not feel buried or overwhelmed in the moment...but to deliver a true to life read on the mood of the room and play off that energy...

Our music is like a favored hiking path...we know the trail so well... but at the same time we look for and find something new each time we pass...at times we go off road...beyond the trail...finding our way as we go...each time making new pathways and passages...always with the same destination in mind...to find and see beauty, danger, intrigue, and to safely find our way back every time."

Inside the World of Mr. J

Joe Henderson: The Last Word

"As we as a culture move forward towards new music frontiers, the history of the long-gone past of America's African musical roots and beginnings must be remembered and passed along. This is, after all, what gives Jazz its authenticity.

Only when we have begun to respect the great diversity of our global culture will we human beings truly create enduring societies.

The Jazz ensemble might well be the best place to witness, firsthand, the building of a peaceful and creative dialogue between humans."

~ From a letter to Harrison Goldberg
  April 15, 1996

A National American Treasure

H.CON.RES 57: Jazz is a "National American Treasure"
Passed by the 100th Congress of the United States of America
Introduced by the Honorable John Conyers Jr.

Whereas, jazz has achieved preeminence throughout the world as an indigenous American music and art form, bringing to this country and the world a unique American musical synthesis and culture through the African American experience and

> 1. makes evident to the world an outstanding artistic model of individual expression and democratic cooperation within the creative process, thus fulfilling the highest ideals and aspirations of our republic,
> 2. is a unifying force, bridging cultural, religious, ethnic and age difference in our diverse society,
> 3. is a true music of the people, finding its inspiration in the cultures and most personal experiences of the diverse peoples that constitute our Nation,
> 4. has evolved into a multifaceted art form which continues to birth and nurture new stylistic idioms and cultural fusions,
> 5. has had an historic, pervasive and continuing influence on other genres of music both here and abroad, and
> 6. has become a true international language adopted by musicians around the world as a music best able to express contemporary realities from a personal perspective;

Whereas, this great American musical art form has not yet been properly recognized nor accorded the institutional status commensurate with its value and importance;

Whereas, it is important for the youth of America to recognize and understand jazz as a significant part of their cultural and intellectual heritage;

Whereas, in as much as there exists no effective national infrastructure to support and preserve jazz;

Whereas, documentation and archival support required by such a great art form has yet to be systematically applied to the jazz field; and

Whereas, it is now in the best interest of the national welfare and all of our citizens to preserve and celebrate this unique art form;

Now, therefore be it Resolved by the House of Representatives (the Senate concurring), that it is the sense of the Congress that jazz is hereby designated as a rare and valuable national American treasure to which we should devote our attention, support and resources to make certain it is preserved, understood and promulgated.

Passed by the House of Representatives: September 23, 1987 and the Senate: December 4, 1987

Bird's Land

APPENDIX

Acknowledgments

The making of this book (including original art pieces) and the quest tale I have crafted for it, have had their fair share of magical occurrences, enough so that at times I felt like the story was writing itself.

Once, at an exhibit at San Francisco's Museum of Modern Art, I came across a painting in a series by the artist Sigmar Polke entitled "The Spirits That Lend Strength Are Invisible." I kept coming back to this compelling title which, over the years since I first viewed the image, has continued to provoke thought, especially when I have assessed the factors, seen and unseen, that have contributed to any works of art I have personally created. While I concur in the premise that some of the magic that occurs in one's creative explorations may be attributed to numinous, and as yet unexplained phenomena, the importance of empirical knowledge is concrete and indisputable and has also helped shape and bring this book project to fruition.

In the City of New Bedford, Massachusetts, where I grew up, rich cultural and musical influences informed my path. Along with accompanying my mother's piano at home, playing jazz standards and Broadway show tunes, I began gigging professionally during the 1960's with the Spindle City 5 from Fall River, MA, and later with the Manhattans, a hometown group. All this was the crucible where I forged my early jazz musical identity and development. African American, Cape Verdean and Portuguese also found a way into the improvisational language of my personal musical expression, consequently engendering my world view of inclusiveness that underlies this tale.

I am grateful to Coleman Hawkins, the father of the jazz tenor saxophone, whose personal story and unmistakably compelling sound presaged the rich African American music history peopled with inspirational saxophone practitioners, past and present. These musicians first captured my imagination and continue to inspire, teach, guide, and help mold the next generation of aspiring jazz players into seasoned musicians.

For my jazz brother, Berklee College of Music classmate and fellow saxophonist, Jim Kingsby, the inspiration for the story's narrator, Forest Tune, I am appreciative. Your friendship, enthusiasm shared for the music we love, and your wise counsel helped this then musical novice keep his ship on course while navigating the turbulent waters of our college's often challenging curriculum.

When I had the opportunity to meet him and share creative ideas surrounding my work, Joe Henderson, the late jazz tenor saxophone titan and educator, understood my imperative to present an impressionable mentor figure for my story. Over a period of five years, a series of in-person conversations with Mr. Henderson ultimately became the basis for the character of Dr. Saxx who occupies a principal role in the story as the mentor of the jazz saxophonist aspirant, Stormy Keys. In addition, my friend and fellow saxophonist, Phillipe Vieux, generously shared saxophone tips gleaned from some lessons he took with Mr. Henderson. To avoid any unwarranted association with the character, Dr. Sax, in Jack Kerouac's novel "Dr. Sax," my friend, Marilyn Boehl, suggested an obvious and much appreciated solution to the naming of this story's mentor; "why not add a second 'x' to his name." And thus, Dr. Saxx sprang to life!

I am equally indebted to the following other real-life mentors who, along the road, have peopled my musical, literary and visual art journey, and directly or indirectly inspired, informed and/or influenced the writing of this tale. It is no small feat to remember all these individuals from near and far who have had an impact on my creative life, but I feel that it is my obligation for the generous gift of encouragement I have received to pay everyone their just due: my brother, Dr. Alan Goldberg, my grandfather Leo Shality, my uncles Dr. Leo Goldberg and Donald Moffett, my aunts Belle Berman, Frieda Dovner and Eunice Moffett, my cousins: the Pomerantz family, Andy Russakoff and the Bermans and Dovners, Myron Goldberg; Louis Perry, Dr. Walter Bonner, Andrew Meyer, Gordon Brown, Joe Pykosz, the esteemed crew and Friends of the S.S. Nobska, Lionel Soares, Avelino "Young Boboi" Soares, the Linden Brothers, George Joblin, Gene Oliver, Eddie "Stack" Ames, Carol and Lou Karajohn, Jim "Red" Carr, Frank

Cornwall, Jimmy Church, Cassius Tandy, the Borowski family, Frank Groh, Everett Hoagland, Jackie Byard, Glen Ingram, Keith Husbands, Mahler Ryder, Andy McGhee, Bill Pierce, Hartley Severns, David Amram, Gene and Leslie Hanson, and Arnie Krakowsky.

Others encountered on my journey include: Porfirio Sorse, Dave of Friends Music, Westport, MA, the Moss Music Store family, Newport, R.I., Coqui Ramirez, Wing Ming Chow, Diego Jameau, Alexander Barry, Richard Abarno, Elaine Lorrilard, Del Long, Fred Long, Sr., and the Long family, Derwood "Fud" Lesh, Diane Alexander, Ron Main, Ron Reinhardt, Robb Clarke Murphy, Michael Walsh, Katie and Joya Hoyt, Mark Top, Spencer MacLeish, Matthew Quinn, Leppy McCarthy, David Ray, Geoffrey Sullivan, Billy Rose, Alix Smets, W. Lincoln Mossop III, Ron and Rona Lowenstein, Bob Pires, Dennis Maloney, Alan Grassel, Ken Witcher, David Manuel, Art Manchester, Diane Thomas, David Edwards, Jane Iandola, Ron Manville, T.C. Brown, Rick Salas, Joe Field, Sean Callery, John and Nancy Silva Braga, Rick Britto, Michael Cardoza, Tom Reid, Randy Tavares, Michael "Tunes" Antunes, and Gino Micheletti.

Gratitude also to Jules and Irene Faoro, Kathryn and Aron Tomaroff, Merilyn Lafferty, Barbara and Paul Felton, Lynne Monroe and Frank Whittemore, Jim, Ellen and Mark Hodos, Art and Penny Dreyer, Mary Beth Blanchard, Mrs. E.W. Trafford, the Lacey family, John and Betty Hergesheimer, Nadenia Newkirk, Dennis and Darlene Lefler, Yoshiko and Russell Olsen, Margaret and Conrad Levasseur, Susan Ax and James Van Wert, Tony Bigham, Philippe Vieux, the crew at the Last Record Store, Santa Rosa, CA, Gary Meierhenry, Tim Ellis, Steve Hanson, Steve Hoffman, Tom and Brenda Simoneau, Alan Weintraub, Jim Stout, Jim and Gail Moore, Gail and Ron Unzelman, Tracey and Mitch Hawkins, Toni Galli-Sterling, Tammy Boatwright, Paul and Jennifer Tincknell, Natalie Leuthi-Peterson, Fritz Trippel and Vera, Hans Ueli Gerber, Solace Sheets, Otis Zachary and the Buffalo Soldiers, Martin Hudson, the Lane-Chamberlain family, C. Cary and Susie Lindsay, Rich and Suzanne Tuttle, Lee Webb, Robert McCurdy, Robin Eschner, Law Offices of Jeannette M. Boudreau, Irene Williams, Frank Gladstone, Billie Youn, Dona Zemo, "Hershel," Rockne Krebs, Christo and

Jeanne-Claude, J. H. Peterson, Carl and Kathy Hersh, Barbara and Andrew Capitman, Albert Bildner, Gil Evans, Clark Terry and Willie Ruff, and Asha Carolyn Young. To Linda and Morgan Lambert, thanks for believing in me.

I want to thank Steve Miller, Ron Thompson, Troy Silveira, Roger Foote, Richard Royea, John Fairweather of Pres Records, Terkild Vinding, Ann and Bob Frowick, Micah Schwaberow, Sandy and Lauren Thompson, Jimmy Brock, Jim Boggio, Fred Lamberson, Eric Drake of Saxcraft in Berkeley, CA, Rex Olsen, Richard Carter, Fred Adler, Violet Arana, David "Sus" and Harmony Susalla, Barbara Pratt, Mark Hancock, P.D. Serratoni, David and Dolly Steffen of the Lighthouse Peddler, the staff of the Independent Coast Observer, Gualala, CA., Saundra Brewer, Greg and Azuza Hagin, Lucinda Weaver and Matthias Oppliger, Alan Bern, Heidi and Don Endemann, John Simon Burnett and Ursula Hamilton, Paul Schulte, Jason Caselli, Philip Barlow, Michael Beattie, Rohesia Hamilton Metcalfe, Robert Hantzsche, Dave Jordan, P.T. Nunn, Lynn Stoller, Janet DeBar, Gretchen Barton, Leon Schneiderman and Mindy Eisman, Zoë Presley, Ian and Amanda Stinson, Peter Mullins of Stone Zone, Michael Burton, Jeanie Dooha, Jim and Akiko Docker, Jerry "Dancer" Erickson, Seve Cardosi, Brian Frost, Andy Lang, Harvey and Sharon Mendelson of Gold Coast Digital and Red Shoes Gallery, Santa Rosa, CA, Terri Spenst, Matt Krumme, Marlene Gay, Lillian Mattimore, Paulette Staker, Marcos Underwood, Ylonda Nickell, Keelyn O'Brien, Kenny Washington, Matt and Gail Taylor, Ledia Carlsen and Bob Schwartz, Phillip and Massomeh Roberts, and from Point Arena, CA: Elijah Carreiro, Tim Lum and Barbara Burkey of 215 Main, Lena Bullamore, Blake More, Lauren Synnott, Joyce Schowengerdt, Jeff Hillier of Think Visual Art Gallery, and Phil Marrinan, Elisabeth Gladstone, Ron and Rukmini Das of MendoVine´, Gualala, CA, and Jake Stillman of Stillman Sound.

I've also shared the stage with: Rick Fulkerson, Gary Pasqualetti, Chris Brady, Mike Roche, Tom Landecker, Kash Killion, Andy Graham, John Gilmore, Kiyoshi "Ken" Tokunaga, Richard Cooper, Rob Ellis, Jesse Bessoni, Lincoln Andrews and Michael Cantwell, Scott Foster, Steve Weber, Joel Kruzic, Colin Hogan, Nils Molin, Gino Raugi, Joel Bennett, Lenny Kaplan and Bippy McMaster, Noah and Sebastian Kaplan, Chris Campbell, James

"Purple" Hayes, Sita Milchev, David and Lucienne Allen and family, Brynn Harris, Don Watanabe, Eric Kritz, Don Krieger, Teo Ariola, Tom Shader, Danny Barca, Pete Gealey, Dorian and Dorothea May, Gabe Yanez, Charlie Valle, Karl Young, Johny Qwest Heubel, Doug O'Connor, the Jazz Beat Poet Ruth Weiss, Alma Owens and Bill Delucchi, Greg Hester, Steve Della Maggiore and Charles Lang. And to my Baku bandmates: Chris Doering, Tim Mueller, Nancy Feehan, and David French—thanks for the awesome music of our inspired creative collaboration.

Others who have inspired this artist's creative journey, while far too numerous to be recorded herein, are respectfully remembered and celebrated. All that each one of you freely gave from your heart has kept me motivated and connected to the craft of jazz music, writing and visual art.

To assist this West Coast transplant in providing the story with some real-life locations in 1960's era New York City, I turned to Bob Farkas, a friend and New Yorker, who graciously accepted the task and subsequently put boots on the ground to contribute a number of authentic settings. His efforts are greatly appreciated.

As anyone who has ever written and published well knows, the process of editing, while remaining synchronistic with and true to the writer's literary intent and original style, is by no means an easy task for either the writer or editor. That being said, I have looked to my sister, Risa Goldberg, for her patient counsel and editing acumen to polish a variety of essays and poetry randomly delivered to her over the years. Needless to say, I have always been appreciative and pleased with the results she has achieved on my behalf. A talented musician, writer and gardener in her own right, I am once again grateful that Risa has expertly pruned my tangled garden of word weeds in this manuscript.

And in Gualala, California, this tiny Mendocino County coastal community that I call home, I am equally indebted to Diana Hillmer of Office Source, whose timely and professional graphics work has been indispensable to this and a host of other creative endeavors I have pursued over the years. And it should go without saying that our community is grateful for her knowledge and the services she and her business provide.

I also express heartfelt gratitude to Donna Bishop for her healing wisdom, the way she listens to flora and fauna, and how she shares the knowledge.

A special shout-out and thank you to Erin Riley and John Crowley, the best fans "evah!" Our long-lasting friendship, a shared love of jazz music and your unselfish support for me, especially during some challenging times, have made this project possible.

Finally, a lifelong passion and personal love of jazz music has defined and given substance to my life for which I am extremely grateful. All of it: the journey, the road, practice sessions, recording opportunities, long-lasting friendships with musicians and listeners alike, this indefatigable quest to become a jazz saxophonist toting his case with the serpent-shaped Excalibur within from gig to gig, it's all in my story. Listen to Jazz and thrive!

~ In gratitude,

Harrison Goldberg: A Biography

Harrison Goldberg, this book's author and illustrator, is also a professional jazz saxophonist. Growing up in a musical family his first musical influence was listening to his Mother's piano as she belted out Broadway show tunes. He would eventually go on to regularly accompany her on saxophone. A love of reading encouraged by his Father inspired and helped develop the author's writing skills and style. While still a teenager, an unexpected clandestine visit to a jazz club exposed Goldberg to the tenor saxophone and live music—and the die was cast. A lifetime love for jazz and the strong desire to become a professional musician ensued, defining the author's personal journey to find his Holy Grail of artistic expression.

The impressionable jazz neophyte would ultimately attend Boston's famed Berklee College of Music and settle for a time in Newport, RI, where he became a fixture on the local jazz club scene and at high visibility events such as The America's Cup and Tall Ships celebrations. He also performed on Caribbean cruise ships and in the famed Art Deco Hotels of Miami Beach, Florida.

To introduce children to the wonderful world of music, Harrison took an innovative and unique approach with a fable he crafted and applied through interactive music workshops in Libraries and Day Care Centers throughout New England. His original story transformed the terms and symbols of music theory into characters and settings in an imaginary landscape, creatively holding the children's rapt attention.

As a self-taught visual artist with a unique graffiti-like style, Goldberg has enjoyed a number of high-profile exhibits, and some of his work has found its way into international collections. Recently, as a founding member of the jazz group *duo'Xplore*, he collaborated on an immersive visual and music project titled "dream smuggler", featuring an Artbook with selections of Goldberg's visual art. For more info on this project visit: duoxplore.art

The Certainty of Uncertainty: painting eclectic, riffing poetic, another Artbook project currently underway, is a collaboration with a contemporary poet whose 58 poems form the literary expression of an equal number of Goldberg's paintings. Selections of Goldberg's visual art, as well as his full music discography can be viewed at HarrisonGoldbergArts.com

The author attributes his diverse creativity to "an eclectic life shaped by an exposure to colorful experiences and people." He has at times been a newsboy on a steamship, factory worker in a textile mill, journalist in the US Army, a longshoreman, bartender, haberdashery salesman, and most recently a wine broker and aspiring wine label designer. Through it all Harrison has been true to his love and professional pursuit of jazz, and he continues to record and perform extensively from his coastal home base in Northern California.

Once Upon a Tune: An Inspired Collaboration

When two or more musicians get together for the first time to play jazz, the common vocabulary of the improvisational language they speak instantly creates familiarity, although the interpretation of the music most often represents differing points of view. When personal expression in the service of a shared goal unfolds in real time, that's what jazz is all about.

The design and creation of this book, in a process much like playing jazz, owes its genesis to the creative spontaneity, collaboration and evolution between myself (writer, illustrator and jazz saxophonist) and Connie King, the artistic and gifted creative director/designer who guided the publishing process of *Once Upon a Tune.*

Riffing, ruminating and rhythm-a-ning, we believe we have arrived at an elegant and accessible book, its pages embellished with original paintings, designs and collages. The story's interwoven threads of friendship, perseverance, mentorship, and brotherhood speak to the Democratic ideals that jazz music espouses.

Dear Reader, may this, our shared creative endeavor, inspire, inform and bring you much pleasure.

www.ingramcontent.com/pod-product-compliance
Lightning Source LLC
Chambersburg PA
CBHW040051020826
48978CB00020B/119